KT-549-424

CHASING DANGER

Bromley Libraries

30128 80246 595 8

Scholastic Children's Books
An imprint of Scholastic Ltd
Euston House, 24 Eversholt Street,
London, NW1 1DB, UK
Registered office: Westfield Road, Southam,
Warwickshire, CV47 0RA

SCHOLASTIC and associated logos are trademarks and/or
registered trademarks of Scholastic Inc.

First published in the UK by Scholastic Ltd, 2016

Text copyright © Sara Grant, 2016

The right of Sara Grant to be identified as the author of
this work has been asserted by her.

ISBN 978 1407 16329 1

A CIP catalogue record for this book is available from
the British Library. All rights reserved.

This book is sold subject to the condition that it shall not,
by way of trade or otherwise, be lent, hired out or otherwise
circulated in any form of binding or cover other than that in which
it is published. No part of this publication may be reproduced,
stored in a retrieval system, or transmitted in any form or by any
means (electronic, mechanical, photocopying, recording or
otherwise) without prior written permission of Scholastic Limited.

Printed by CPI Group (UK) Ltd, Croydon, CR0 4YY
Papers used by Scholastic Children's Books are made from wood grown
in sustainable forests.

1 3 5 7 9 10 8 6 4 2

This is a work of fiction. Names, characters, places, incidents
and dialogues are products of the author's imagination or are used
fictitiously. Any resemblance to actual people, living or dead,
events or locales is entirely coincidental.

www.scholastic.co.uk

TO PAUL. FOR ALL OUR ADVENTURES TOGETHER
AND THE ONES YET TO COME.

1

"Don't leave me here!" I shouted and waved wildly at the seaplane as it floated away with a roar and spray of salty water.

I was standing on a twelve-by-twelve floating dock in the middle of the Indian Ocean. I had survived twenty hours trapped on planes – forty-five minutes of that on a seaplane – and then me and my bags had been abandoned here. My brain and mouth felt fuzzy from recycled air and plastic plane food.

"Come back!" I screamed as the plane cut a wide

arc in the water, preparing to take off again. If it left, I would be stuck here. Nowhere to run. Nowhere to hide. Panic punched me in the gut.

Maybe the pilot couldn't see me. I jumped as high as I could while simultaneously screeching at the top of my lungs. Bad idea. The dock tilted, and I staggered to the edge. I flailed my arms to regain my balance, but I was out of sync with the bobbing dock. My backpack and duffle slid towards me. I had to do something quickly or they'd be tossed into the ocean.

I lunged forward and landed face first on my bags, spreadeagle in the centre of the dock. I'd saved my stuff from a watery grave. Relief flooded through me, but only for the briefest of seconds. I flipped over in time to see the seaplane zoom past and take flight.

"Noooooooooooooooooooooooo!" I sprang to my feet. Another bad idea.

The plane's wake rocked the dock. I was catapulted into the air. There was absolutely nothing I could do. I screamed as I plunged butt-first into the ocean. Big mistake. The sound was strangled by gallons of water splashing over me.

What had my dad told me NEVER to do in an emergency? Oh, yeah – panic.

Too late.

My lungs burned for air. My short, pathetic life flashed before my eyes, but maybe that was only a school of fish because my life wasn't that colourful. I needed to calm down, which wasn't easy when you lacked oxygen and were waging an epic battle with the Indian Ocean.

I clawed my way to the surface and gulped in air. Two strokes and I was back at the dock. Thankfully my luggage had only shifted to the edge and hadn't toppled in. I flopped on the dock and let the hot sun dry my drenched clothes. I combed my fingers through my seaweed-like hair and twisted it in a knot at the back of my head, securing it with the rubber band I always keep around my wrist. I felt a bit wobbly after my almost-sort-of-near-death experience. My fear quickly drained away and was replaced by an all too familiar feeling – annoyance.

All I'd had to do was stand still and wait. I couldn't even do that right.

The sky and ocean merged into an uncomfortable blanket of blue around me. The sun created ripples of liquid diamonds in the water. It was beautiful in a last-man-standing-after-the-apocalypse way. The gentle swaying and the whisper of the waves should have been soothing. Some people might have found the quiet and vast nothingness peaceful, but I couldn't help feeling that I'd made a massive mistake.

When Dad told me about this trip to the Maldives, I was actually excited. He was ex-United States Navy so my life had been a fourteen-year-long boot camp. He'd been recruited for some big assignment at the Pentagon for a month, maybe two. He needed somewhere to dump me. A desert island getaway sounded pretty amazing. While my friends were slaving away in the snowy January cold, I'd be soaking up the sun and exploring the sea. Now standing smack-dab in the middle of nowhere, I knew that I hadn't escaped, only changed prisons.

The sun's rays singed my skin like thousands of searing hot needles. After only five minutes, my clothes were nearly dry. Maybe it was my imagination, but my pasty white skin appeared a shade pinker.

If the heat didn't kill me then I might die of boredom. I had found a crumpled copy of the island's glossy brochure shoved between the seaplane's seat cushions. It boasted – BOASTED – no wifi, TVs or phones. And if that wasn't bad enough, the resort catered exclusively to senior citizens. Dad had left out those two very important details. The most active item on the island's itinerary was water aerobics. I didn't want to think of wrinkly bingo wings flapping about in the pool.

I could deal with heat and boredom, but the thing that was causing the complete and utter meltdown of my internal organs was meeting my British grandma for the first time. I imagined she looked like the Queen of England. I didn't know for sure because I'd never seen a picture of my grandma. Until a month ago, I never knew she existed. I mean, I knew everyone had a biological mom, and my mom had a mom, but my dad refused to talk about them.

I'd suspected I was adopted, kidnapped, and at one point, cloned. My dad had assured me that he was my father, and I was conceived the old-fashioned way. *Gross!* I'd interrogated, snooped, tricked and begged. He never uttered one syllable about the person who donated her egg nor did I ever find one shred of evidence that she was really real. I had sort of learned to accept my mysterious lack of mom. But today my family tree would expand by one branch whether I liked it or not, and I was freaking out. I couldn't remember why I'd ever wanted to meet the old woman who'd never tried to see me or even send me so much as a birthday text.

I checked my phone. The screen was blank. Water dribbled out of the charging and headphone slots. I stabbed at the buttons and poked at the screen. It was dead. I knew how to perform CPR, but I had no idea how to resuscitate a drenched, lifeless cell phone. The first casualty of my so-called vacation. I had a feeling it wouldn't be the last.

At least my watch was waterproof. It said it was about six o'clock in the morning, but that was Indiana time. I'd lost two days travelling. There was a nine-hour time difference between Indiana and the Maldives so that would make it three in the afternoon.

I searched for any sign of life. I didn't know if I was being picked up by speedboat or jetpack. Something in the distance was moving towards me.

Was that. . . ?

Nah, don't be ridiculous.

I stood and squinted. Maybe it was the curl of a wave. I stepped closer to the edge. No, that was definitely a fin cutting through the water.

SHARK!

I was a sitting duck on this platform. I imagined the jaws of a Great White chomping me and the dock with one ginormous bite. While I was packing my swimsuit, sunscreen, bug spray and three graphic novels, sharks didn't enter my mind. Sharks were only in movies and wildlife TV shows. They didn't target fresh US prime-cut kids.

That fin was definitely swimming closer. There was no use calling for help because no one would hear me. I staggered back, tripped on my duffle, and fell hard on my butt. My hands splashed in the water behind me. I scuttled forward. I wasn't going back in what I now knew were shark-infested waters.

I ransacked my duffle for something I could use as a weapon. Could you blind a shark with toothpaste? I didn't have straighteners or a hairdryer or any beauty products that might contain shark-repelling chemicals. If only I was more girlie – that way I'd at least have had hairspray, tweezers or stilettos. I dug through my shorts, flip-flops, and a rainbow-collection of T-shirts from bike races and fun runs. I found nothing I could use to defend myself. I was shark bait, plain and simple.

I braced myself as the fin dipped lower and arched closer. This was it. I was going to die and no one would ever know what happened to me. Tomorrow's newspaper headline would read:

Charlotte 'Chase' Armstrong Disappears Without a Trace.

The water erupted in front of me. A sound clawed at my throat until I was all-out horror-movie shrieking.

I stopped mid-scream as my brain told my body what my eyes had actually seen.

The creature burst from the water again and I got a better look.

A dolphin.

My fear melted like a vanilla-chocolate twist in the August heat of the State Fair. I'd never heard of death by dolphin. I was such an idiot. I laughed as three dolphins jumped and twisted giving me my very own SeaWorld show. As they raced away, I repacked my duffle. My dad would be so disappointed. He'd raised me to take care of myself, and I'd freaked at a dolphin swim-by. Dad had made me practise fire drills and obstacle courses. He showed me aikido so I could manoeuvre out of any chokehold or defend against a backpack thief. He never told me what to do in case of a shark attack. In his defence, we lived in Indiana where the chances of seeing a shark – outside of an aquarium – were less than zero.

I found my sunglasses at the bottom of my backpack and slipped them on. Between the scratches on the lenses and the waves, I thought I saw a boat heading towards me. I should have felt relieved. I wasn't going to drown or die by shark attack, or shrivel under the baking sun, or simply be left to suffer starvation and dehydration. But I couldn't shake the feeling that this vacation might actually kill me.

I was rescued, but that uneasy feeling swirled around me like a hurricane in a fishbowl. The boat that puttered up to the floating dock looked like a mini Viking ship without the massive sails or the guys in horned helmets.

"Hello, Charlotte!" an older grey-haired man called from the approaching boat. He was pastier and whiter than I was. A young, tanned, shirtless guy was steering the big wooden wheel at the front of the boat.

"Hi," I waved. No one called me Charlotte. "It's

Chase," I corrected. He smiled and nodded in a way that meant he couldn't hear me or couldn't care less. At least I wasn't alone in the universe any more.

A mermaid was carved into the bow of the boat and stretched from sea level past the roof and reached the dock first. I had to duck to avoid being whacked by the mermaid when the boat swung parallel to me with surprising precision.

The old guy scanned me from head to toe. His nose wrinkled as if he whiffed something nasty. I'd been travelling and hadn't seen my reflection for twenty-four hours. My blue *Race for Life* T-shirt was damp and rumpled. I placed my hand over the Coke stain on my shorts from when we'd hit turbulence over Saudi Arabia. I tried to smooth the kinks from my hair and tightened the knot to make it look somewhat styled instead of the tangled just-out-of-bed-serial-killer mess it usually was. I shrugged in a half apology and half *whatever* way.

This resort was supposed to be some laid-back getaway, but the old guy looked ready for a business meeting. His grey hair was slicked back. I couldn't tell if he'd been swimming or if he over-gelled. He was wearing a perfectly pressed white shirt and khaki trousers.

"Welcome to. . ." I thought he said Mal-Horrific-Shoe-La. I'd seen the name of the island spelled out; it had far too many vowels together for me to be able to pronounce it.

"Thanks," I said, because I thought I should say something.

"I'm Artie, the resort manager." He extended his hand and I shook it. "The island motto is: *No shoes. No news.* We give our over-sixties clientele a complete escape from the outside world." He pointed at my bags, and the young man tossed them in the boat. "I'll have to ask you to be on your best behaviour and not to disturb the other guests. . ."

He kept talking about rules that basically meant I could only whisper and tiptoe. Be seen and not heard. His British accent made him sound smarter and made me feel dumber. Two big thumbs down for old people resorts. So far my vacation sucked with a capital SU – and I hadn't reached the island yet!

"Ready?" he asked and held out his hand to help me aboard as if I was some damsel in distress. *I don't think so.* I launched myself into the boat. I'd won the high jump on sports day so I landed dead centre. The boat rocked and Artie was knocked back on to one of the benches along the side. He scowled at me. "I think we are ready to leave now, Luke."

Luke gave me a sneaky wink and tried to hide his smile from Artie.

Artie began to tap on his cell phone. I guessed my welcome was officially over.

I stepped up next to Luke. "So what's the real deal with this place?" I whispered to him.

He pointed to the island that was coming into focus. It looked tiny from here. A green blob of palm trees ringed with a beach of white sand. My grandma was on that island, and so was the truth – if I was brave enough to ask. Maybe it was time to solve the mystery of my mom.

"The island is basically a triangle with the boat dock on one point, the Aquatic Centre for our range of recreational water activities on the middle point, and the overwater bungalows on the final point. See how the water is a lighter shade of blue between the boat dock and the bungalows?" Luke gestured to the area right ahead of us.

I nodded. I'd call that colour Blizzard Blue from the fluorescent Crayola crayons collection.

"A natural reef surrounds half the island and creates a massive lagoon." I could tell English wasn't his first language. He spoke every word precisely as if mimicking the voices on those language apps. "You should go snorkelling. The coral and sea life are magnificent. Flippers and goggles are provided in every bungalow." It sounded like he'd given this speech before.

"That sounds amazing." I'd only ever swum in swimming pools or murky lakes. Oranges, yellows and reds flickered in the water below. I couldn't wait to go underwater exploring without my dad making me sit out for fifteen minutes every hour, or telling me to stay close to the shore, or not dive so deep. "What about sharks?"

Luke laughed. "We have lots of sharks. Most are harmless. The reef creates a natural barrier so none of the big ones can swim into the lagoon. If you want to explore outside the reef," he pointed to two yellow flags that looked like the ones Dad put on the back of my first bike, "that's the only place you can safely cross the reef through a gap in the coral. The sea creatures are more spectacular on the dark side of the reef. Stay alert. Sharks generally won't bother you if you don't provoke them."

"Check! No provoking sharks," I replied. I wasn't exactly sure how you might provoke a shark. Make fun of its fin? Flick it on the nose? If I saw a shark, I planned to swim the other way as fast as my flippers would take me.

"Can you hurry it up?" Artie barked at Luke. "I've got better things to do than babysit."

Ouch!

"Yes, sir," Luke said, and shifted the boat into high gear. His face changed from soft and smiley to stone. I could see his lips moving. I couldn't hear what he said over the roar of the engine, but I could tell it wasn't nice by the way he glared at Artie out of the corner of his eye.

We sailed closer to the island, and I understood why the rich and famous escaped to places like this. It was completely secluded; the perfect tropical island paradise. It was no bigger than four or five football fields. The overwater bungalows Luke had mentioned were at the far end of the island. I counted twenty of them attached to a long wooden pier and suspended on stilts over the lagoon.

"Wow," I muttered. My skin tingled with goosebumps. I hadn't really thought about where I'd be sleeping. Even if the island was only for old people, it was going to be pretty awesome staying in one of those. They each had their own private deck and steps that lead straight into the lagoon. For the first time since my plane took off from Indianapolis, I felt a glimmer of hope. If dear old Granny Sinclair was crazy, evil or hated my guts from the moment she laid eyes on me, at least I could still snorkel every day and enjoy the sunshine.

As we approached the boat dock, Luke expertly manoeuvred around the row boats and Jet Skis that were tethered there. Artie was off the boat the second it came to a complete stop.

"Come on!" he shouted at me. I flinched at the nasty tone in his voice. "I mean, we are ever so pleased you're here." His tone softened and his lips curled into a weird, tight smirk. "Ariadne asked that I take you to her as soon as you arrived."

Ariadne. That was her name. Was I really going to meet my long-lost granny? Waves of worry sloshed through my veins.

Luke was busy tying the boat to the dock. Artie checked his phone again and made no move to help me with my things – not that I wanted his stupid help. I looped my backpack on one shoulder and hugged my duffle to my chest. I stepped up on the bench and teetered on the rail of the boat before staggering forward and nearly face-planting on the dock.

The dock extended into the dark side of the reef, as Luke had called it. I stared down at the rocky channel that ran parallel to the long walkway. The water below bubbled and frothed like a hot tub. I leaned forward for a better look and gasped. Two creatures, which appeared to be part dragon and part snake, were pretzelled together and attacking anything that so much as twitched.

Artie frowned at my outburst and placed his pointer finger on his lips. The universal sign for *shut up*.

"Sorry," I said.

He looked in the water to see what had startled me. "We call them Twist and Shout."

"Yeah, but what are they?" I grimaced at the thought of swimming in the same ocean as those thick snakes with pointy snouts.

"Haven't you seen an eel before?" he asked, as if I was the stupidest kid on the planet. "They patrol the reef. It's best to steer clear of them." He pivoted on his Jesus sandals. "Follow me!" he called as he marched down the long pier to the island.

I struggled to keep up. He was doing this weird race walk. I felt the weight of every mile I'd travelled and every ounce of my luggage. Sweat dripped down my temples and created dark polka dots on my T-shirt. I had hoped to change into something less bag-lady or at least wash my face before I met my grandma. Maybe the quick, accidental dip in the ocean had washed away a bit of the no-shower and airplane stench.

"Ariadne prefers the sun in the yoga studio at this time of day," Artie explained as we walked to a pavilion with a veranda around it. Sheer white curtains fluttered in the ocean breeze from floor-to-ceiling windows.

That jittery, nervous feeling that had been building all day eased when I noticed the old woman reclining in a lounge chair on the veranda wearing a simple floral sundress and reading a thick novel. She looked like the text-book definition of grandma with white hair swept into a neat bun and glasses perched on the end of her nose. When we reached the veranda, I dropped my bags, stashed my sunglasses and checked my reflection in a window. I unlooped the rubber band and rumpled my hair until it was the good kind of messy. I tugged on the hem of my T-shirt to minimize the wrinkles, but it was no use. I looked exactly like what I was: someone who had been travelling for forty-eight hours then been dunked in the ocean, tossed on a boat and dragged across a sandy desert island.

Artie noticed I'd fallen behind. "What are you doing?"

The old woman looked up and gave me this warm, grandmotherly smile. I gathered my courage and stepped forward. "I'm—" I started but Artie interrupted.

"That's not Ariadne." He turned to the old lady. "Sorry for the interruption, Mildred." Embarrassment singed me from the inside out. I should have known we weren't related. She seemed too normal and nice to be my mysterious grandma. He grabbed my wrist and led me into the yoga studio.

In the middle of the room, reflected in the wall of mirrors, was unmistakably my grandma. It was as if I was looking at one of those apps that it ages a picture of you by fifty years. She had short-spikey white hair. Her legs were in a sturdy lunge and her arms extended straight over her head. I knew from my yoga classes in PE that she was striking the warrior pose. She wore black yoga pants with a neon green cami. There was not a bingo wing – or an ounce of flab – in sight. She was in better shape than I was.

She finally noticed me in the mirror. She didn't flinch from her pose. For a long second, we stared at the other's reflection.

"We meet at last," she said.

3

I stood there, open-mouthed, like a stupid doll begging for a cuddle. What did you say to the grandma who didn't pause her yoga to greet the granddaughter she'd never met?

"Artie's doing me a massive favour by letting you stay on the island. I suppose Artie's reviewed the rules with you."

Her gushy, lovey-dovey welcome was overwhelming – NOT!

"If anyone asks, you are my new personal assistant."

No one in a million years would believe I was old enough to have a job. "Sure." I shrugged.

"Please do not," she emphasized the *not* part of the sentence, "call me any version of the word *grandma*." She made what was normally warm and fuzzy sound like a cuss word. "You may call me Ariadne." She stepped back and shifted her position into an upside-down V. "Do you understand, Charlotte?"

"OK," I mumbled. I'd travelled thousands of miles and spent hundreds of hours thinking about this woman. She obviously hadn't wasted one minute thinking of me. Anyone who knew me for more than a minute knew I hated being called Charlotte. "Everyone calls me Chase."

She craned her neck to look up at me. "Chase?" she asked. "Why would they call you that?"

"Dad said from the moment I could crawl," not that she would know anything about my childhood, "he was chasing after me."

"No, I don't think I can call you that," my granny said. "Not very respectable."

So I had to call her Ariadne, but she wouldn't call me Chase. That didn't seem fair.

"Artie, be a dear, and take Charlotte to our bungalow," dear ol' granny continued.

"Chase," I corrected. She ignored me.

Artie transformed into a big mushy puppy dog. "Anything for you, my darling."

I thought I might actually vomit.

Ariadne inhaled and then loudly exhaled as she stood up. She faced me. Even after her cold-to-nearly-freezing welcome, everything in me still wanted to run over and hug her. I wanted to beg her to be my grandma, the kind that makes you feel special or at least liked a teeny tiny bit. But I didn't move.

"I'm sure we'll get along just fine," she said.

"Yeah," I muttered but I wasn't sure she was right, and by the flat tone of her voice, I guessed neither was she.

I whipped around scattering sand over the gleaming wooden floor. I wanted to get out of there as fast as possible and end this awkwardness. I liked her better before we met.

By the time I reached my bungalow on the opposite side of the island at the end of a long wooden pier, I was drenched in sweat and speckled with sand. I was glad that Artie basically shoved me inside and ran away. On the outside, the bungalow appeared pretty basic – like a hut made of driftwood with a grass roof – but inside it transformed into something more like the best suite in some fancy hotel. A speck of dust didn't dare rest on the glass-topped nightstands. No thread frayed from the five-thousand-count Egyptian cotton sheets. The curved sofa and overstuffed armchair looked like no one had ever flopped on them or spilled a drop of orange soda on the creamy magnolia fabric.

I stepped on to my own personal deck. I scanned the island and the lagoon; there was not another person in sight. The only sound was the lapping of the waves against the concrete pillars that held my bungalow over the ocean. I couldn't believe that the hazy sun that made the corn grow in Indiana was the same brilliant glowing ball that was shining down on me now.

A tsunami of self-pity washed over me. I'd hoped that when Ariadne saw me in person she would stop her lifelong granddaughter boycott and actually be pleased to meet her own flesh and blood. Obviously not.

I picked up the room phone and punched in Dad's number. I had never wanted to talk to my dad more than I did right now. I took a deep breath as the phone clicked and buzzed. I needed to make my voice sound normal. He could usually tell my mood in an instant. I didn't want him to know that I was miserable and desperate to be beamed back to my stupid, old, boring room in Indiana.

An automated British female voice answered, "I'm sorry, but your call cannot be completed." Then the rude lady hung up on me.

I was sure I'd dialled the right number. I tried again. The lady delivered the same message.

I definitely needed assistance. I dialled zero as the note on the room phone instructed.

"Hello, Miss Sinclair," another British lady answered but this one was real. "How may I assist you?"

"Um, I'm not Miss Sinclair, I'm Miss Armstrong, I mean, I'm Charlotte but everyone calls me Chase..."

"Hello," the lady said again. "Is everything OK?"

"Yes, I guess," I replied. "I want to call the United States, but this phone won't connect me."

"The phones in the rooms are for internal island calls," she said. "The manager's office has the only external phone on the island."

"Oh..." Why would anyone voluntarily come to an island so cut off from the rest of the world? Without my phone and no access to the internet, I was no better than a prisoner in solitary confinement. My friends would think I was ignoring their texts, chats, messages and posts. I'd have zero friends when Dad broke me out of here.

"Miss Armstrong?" the woman prodded me.

"Oh, nothing." I hung up. I swallowed down my sadness. I could sit here and sulk or ... I had a whole ocean out there to explore.

I slathered myself with sunscreen and slipped on my swimsuit. I kept trying to convince myself that it wasn't so bad. I was in this amazing place, and I could do whatever I wanted. But no matter how hard I tried, the ache of my grandma's rejection wouldn't go away.

I found the snorkelling gear in a wicker basket on the deck. *Suck it up!* I told myself. I'd never been snorkelling before and I was determined to enjoy this once-in-a-lifetime experience. That vast blue ocean was my new playground. Thinking about things would only make me miserable. Doing stuff always made me happy.

As I climbed down the ladder to the lagoon, I felt the same adrenaline rush that I did each time I launched my bike up a ramp for another jump. My feet touched the bath-warm water. I hung the goggles and snorkel around my neck and tugged on the bright yellow flippers. I prepared to fling myself into the water when two eyes blinked up at me from the sandy bottom of the lagoon. I lost my grip and toppled into the water. I curled into a ball so I didn't squash whatever it was below me. A stingray shook away the sand, flicked its arrow-shaped tail and flutter-swam away.

"Wow," I whispered, and snapped the goggles in place. The flippers took a lot of getting used to. They weighed me down and made it more difficult to swim. I fitted the snorkel in my mouth and spluttered at the salty taste. I floated on the surface and practised breathing through the tube. My breath was magnified by the snorkel and drowned out any sound.

Within a few strokes, I was hovering over a huge lump of coral. Creatures of every shape and colour darted around. The coral was nothing like the holey bleached rocks I'd seen in fish tanks. This coral was alive with vibrant greens, pinks and yellows, and swayed in the current.

Every time my brain tried to trick me into feeling sorry for myself, I swam faster and dived deeper. I floated through a school of thousands of tiny nearly see-through fish. As I approached the reef, it was as if my goggles turned into a kaleidoscope. The coral and fish multiplied by the hundreds. I didn't think the colours could be more brilliant, but they were. I surfaced and was surprised at how far away I was from my bungalow now. I'd almost reached the yellow flags Luke pointed out earlier.

The lagoon was about six-feet deep, but the canyon on the other side of the reef seemed dark and endless. I hovered near the flags. My mind did that annoying thing it always does – it thinks of the exact worst thing to think about. It flashed to that old *Jaws* movie poster. The one with the girl splashing happily above, completely unaware that this ginormous shark is heading, jaws open, straight for her.

Sometimes an overactive imagination was a very bad thing. I told myself in my best dad impersonation that I was being silly. I wanted to swim further into the canyon. But my brain kept flipping through images from a shark attack catalogue.

I trod water as a battle between sanity and imagination raged in my head. I was out here alone, and I didn't like the way the depths of the canyon seemed to drag my flippers down.

I didn't feel safe in the water any more. I shut my eyes and swam straight for my bungalow. I pretended I was in the city pool swimming laps. In no time my arm clunked against the railing of the ladder.

I looped the goggles, snorkel and flippers on my arm and climbed up, up, up the ladder. I landed with a splat on the deck. Suddenly my body seemed heavy from the lack of sleep and excessive exercise.

Grandma, I meant Ariadne, must have finished her yoga by now. The sliding door to the bungalow was open and the biggest and fluffiest towel I'd ever seen was tossed on the bright green sunbed. I wrapped the towel around me and collapsed on the lounge chair. I closed my eyes and let the sun warm me.

I was never ever going to get used to calling that woman Ariadne. No one I knew or had ever heard of had that name. It felt unnatural. I practised again. *Ariadne*. Nope, still sounded strange.

The deck creaked. Ariadne must have walked

out to check on me. I wanted to open my eyes but I was drowsy with the sun and the swimming and the hours of travel. I needed a nap and to forget that my grandma was as cuddly as a shark and as warm as an igloo.

I stretched to sitting, slowly opened my eyes – and screamed!

The person looming over me holding a laptop above her head, ready to strike, was not my grandma. The girl was a foot taller than I was, with dark brown skin and spirally reddish-brown curls framing her face like a saint-sized halo. "If you leave now, I won't hurt you!" she shouted with a posh British accent, which made her seem less threatening – that and the fact that she was wearing a bright-red designer bikini.

I scrambled to my feet. She was model thin and perfect except for a jagged scar on her neck. Super-pretty girls didn't usually do daredevil things that left scars. She stepped away but cocked her arms back further, preparing to leave an imprint of the Apple logo on my forehead. Even armed, this girl looked fragile. If push came to shove, I could take her in a fight. "Just relax, Wonder Woman," I said with a nervous laugh.

Big mistake. She narrowed her gaze and screwed her mouth into a threatening scowl. I stepped closer to the ladder.

Then I realized... "What are you doing in my bungalow?" She was the intruder, not me! I twisted the towel between my fists. I could give a pretty good wet-towel burn if I needed to.

"Your bungalow?" she screeched. The sound actually hurt my ears. There was something odd about her expression. I thought she was angry until I recognized that look in her eyes. She was scared. "This is *my* bungalow, and I demand you leave this instant."

The bungalow was the mirror image of Grandma's – Ariadne's. But the twin beds weren't made, and several empty potato chip bags and candy wrappers were scattered on the floor. Her fancy Barbie-sized clothes were thrown everywhere.

I held up my hands in surrender and dropped the towel. "Hey, I'm really sorry. I just got here and I think I used the wrong ladder."

The girl lowered her laptop. "You think?" She relaxed a bit, but her scrawny body still seemed pumped up.

Her room looked like a geek's lair with at least two computers, a printer and some blinking boxes with loads of cables twisting across the floor. A tablet rested on her pillow and was playing something on YouTube. "Hey, I didn't think there was wifi."

The girl switched off her tablet. "Uh, there's not in the bungalows. I found out that the manager's office has it so I've rigged something so I can tap into his wifi for a few hours each day. I've got work to do before I lose my connection." She gestured to the deck. "Do you mind?"

"Not at all," I snapped. Maybe this island emitted

some radiation that made everyone rude. I wished I could have cannonballed off the edge of her deck and soaked her and her stupid computers. Instead I lobbed the wet towel at her and made a clunky exit down the ladder, stubbing my toe as I stomped down.

I eased up the ladder and peered on to the deck of the bungalow next door. Yep, this was the right one. Grandma Ariadne was waltzing around the room in a frilly white sundress that accentuated her golden suntan. She looked completely different than she did in the yoga studio. Her silvery-white hair was feathered towards her face. Her eyes were closed as she swayed to an imaginary orchestra. I didn't really want to interrupt.

"Oh!" Ariadne gasped when she saw my head lurking at deck height like a wet and wild groundhog in search of its shadow. "There you are. It's almost time for dinner. Can you hurry and make yourself presentable?"

I climbed up on to the deck and hugged myself,

suddenly self-conscious of my Walmart swimsuit and, well, everything about me. I stood there dripping, unable to speak.

"Well, get on with it," she said, checking her watch.

I hauled my duffle into the bathroom and did as she had instructed. I returned fifteen minutes later in white combat shorts and my favourite neon-green *Little 500* bike-race T-shirt. My wet hair was slicked back into a ponytail. The only jewellery I owned were watches, and I'd packed seven of my favourites to bring with me. I was wearing a matching green chunky plastic watch with numbers that glowed in the dark.

"Maybe you could wear a dress?" Ariadne asked.

"Uh, I don't really do dresses," I said with an apologetic shrug. Dad had tried to buy me a dress a million times for special occasions. I had one jean skirt, which was the closest he'd ever come to making me somewhat girlie. It wasn't that I didn't want to be fashion-mag pretty. Dresses felt weird on me.

"Oh." Ariadne looked as if she'd been dunked in a vat of disappointment goo. That happened a lot to adults when they were around me. "I can't let you go to dinner looking like some football hooligan." I was pretty sure that was an insult, but I wasn't about to ask her to explain. She rummaged in her closet. "How about this?" She waved a sequined emerald-green, short-sleeved blouse at me.

It wasn't too horrible. I pulled it over my head and wiggled out of my T-shirt. The blouse felt heavy and slightly prickly from the sequins. "Can I wear it with these shorts?" I dug around in my duffle. "And I've got sparkly flip-flops." I held them up for her approval.

"I suppose that will have to do," she said.

As I checked myself out in the hall mirror, Ariadne inspected my appearance too. She took a step towards me. Her delicate perfume whispered that I would never live up to her expensive standards. I froze as she reached up as if she was going to touch my hair. "You look like her," she whispered and lowered her hand.

She said it so quietly, I don't think she intended me to hear. She meant my mom. I stared at my reflection. This tiny spark of information twinkled in my brain. This was my chance to find out something about the other half of my gene pool.

"What is," I swallowed hard, "she like?"

Ariadne squinted at our reflection. I waited and hoped she wouldn't make me ask again. She fidgeted with her hair as if that was more important than my question.

"Tell me about my mother." It was more of a demand than an ask this time.

She walked to her jewellery box and fumbled with a tangle of necklaces and bracelets. "What did your dad tell you about her?"

"Nothing." My voice squeaked. I sounded as desperate as I felt. "He won't talk about her. I don't even know her name."

"Beatrice." She sighed.

My mom's name was Beatrice. I wanted to ask the question that had been burning a hole in me ever since I realized that most kids had two parents, usually a dad and a mom. "Why didn't she. . ." My voice broke. It wasn't just in the past. "Why *doesn't* she want anything to do with me?" The second the words were out, I wanted to take them back. I'd never been able to think of any good answers for that question. Waiting for her reply felt the same as making a monster jump on my bike, the thrill of flight knotted with the fear of the fall.

Ariadne's shoulders hunched as if my question weighed a zillion pounds. She spoke slowly. "She's not a bad person. She was a loving and sweet girl who was well liked at school. She received high marks. She excelled at sports."

My mom was starting to seem real, but Ariadne was avoiding what I really wanted to know. "That's not what I asked."

Ariadne took a deep breath before responding. "She wasn't able to be a mother."

That was a strange thing to say. "Was she too young? Was she ill? Is she dead?" I thought of reasons someone wouldn't be able to be a mother.

Ariadne shook her head. "No, but it's for the best."

My anger took me by surprise. "How can it be for the best?" I shouted.

"Your mum, my daughter, is a complicated woman," she said. There was an edge to her voice. I could tell she wasn't used to anyone yelling at her. "I don't want to talk about this any more," she said, and clipped on a pair of diamond chandelier earrings.

"There's so much I want to know," I begged. For so long, I was half my father and half mystery. A picture of my mom was forming. It was more like a dot-to-dot with big empty spaces.

"Is that the time? We are going to be late for dinner," Ariadne said without looking at her watch. The only conversation I'd ever had about my mom was over. Maybe I could at least get to know Ariadne better over dinner. Maybe I could find some reason to like her, and she could find a tiny reason not to dislike me. "I want you to meet an old family friend," Ariadne told me, as she snatched her silvery pashmina from the bed and headed for the bungalow door. "Come along," she called over her shoulder.

It was obvious Ariadne didn't want to spend time with me. At dinner, she would probably talk with her old friend about wrinkle cream and other old-people stuff. But I'd had my first glimpse of my mother, and now I wanted to know everything – especially the big unspeakable secret that Dad and Grandma didn't want me to find out.

5

I followed Ariadne in silence to the dining hall, feeling the same dread I'd felt on the first day of school. We'd ditched our shoes at the end of the pier and walked barefoot across the island. The dining hall was no more than a thatched roof with a few poles to hold it up and nothing but sand for the floor. It was like an extension of the beach.

"Welcome, Miss Sinclair and Miss Armstrong." It was Luke. I almost didn't recognize him. His dark, wavy hair was combed back and he'd changed into a peach polo shirt and pressed khakis. "Miss Clifford is already waiting for you."

We weaved through the dining room. I was the youngest person here by about fifty years. Ariadne waved at the couples as we passed. "Good evening, Lord and Lady Symington. . . How are you feeling, Sir Charles?" She knew everyone. My grandma was the perfect mash-up of the Queen and a rock star.

These senior citizens were nothing like grandparents in Indiana. You could tell these folks had money. Diamonds were dripping from the women, and the men's wrists gleamed with watches from fancy jewellery stores. I recognized a few of the watch brands and knew that they sold for around $25,000. The most expensive watch in my collection cost $150 and that was only because it was a watch, stopwatch, pedometer and heart monitor in one.

Luke led us to a table set for two at the edge of the dining hall. The setting sun illuminated a pink path almost right to our table. The dishes and glasses were trimmed with gold. I was pretty sure it wasn't the kind that faded in the dishwasher. The dinner plate was outnumbered by eight pieces of silverware and three glasses.

"You?" I said when my focus finally zoomed in on the springy haired girl already seated at the table. "What is she doing here?"

"I'm looking after Miss Clifford for a little while," Ariadne explained.

"You said we were having dinner with an old family friend," I muttered. She wasn't old, not family, and definitely never ever going to be my friend.

"Is *this* your new assistant?" said the girl who had nearly attacked me with a laptop earlier. The tone of her voice let me know that she didn't believe my cover story for one minute.

"Charlotte, this is my dear friend Mackenzie," Ariadne said, pulling out the chair for me.

"She's a kid!" I exclaimed before I could turn on the filter in my brain that blocked stupid things before I blurted them. Yeah, it malfunctioned a lot.

"Am not!" Mackenzie said.

"Are too!"

"I'm fourteen – fifteen next month."

Ariadne looked from me to the girl, confused by our crazy ping-pong match. "Mackenzie is a computer genius." Ariadne laid her hand on the girl's shoulder in a way that made me think they hugged on a daily basis. Maybe it was the green I was wearing but jealousy thumped me in the chest. "In exchange for her guardianship, she's helping me design my *Triple L* app."

I whizzed through the words I could think of that started with L – lonely, loss, loser, labradoodle? "What?"

"It's a dating app for pensioners. I named it Love Late in Life. Mackenzie calls it *Triple L*." Ariadne said it as if the girl had discovered the cure for cancer. It was a stupid nickname. Big deal.

Love Late in Life. I pictured old folks kissing. *EWWWWW!* I was equal parts grossed out and impressed. Downloading apps on my phone was my idea of high tech. This mean girl knew how to make the things.

"I'm going to leave you two girls so you can become better acquainted," Ariadne said, and gave me a little nudge towards the empty seat.

"What?!" The girl and I exclaimed at the same time a bit too loudly. Everyone glared at us.

Ariadne leaned in and whispered, "I need you to be on your best behaviour. It might be nice for you to have a friend your age on the island."

I plopped down on the chair. Why did adults think that if you were the same age and gender you could be friends? The girl and I stared up at Ariadne. We were probably thinking the same thing: *No chance I'm ever going to be friends with her.*

"I invited Artie to a private dinner as a thank you for everything he's done." And with that she floated away without so much as a backward glance. Artie was waiting for her with this silly grin on his face. He looped his arm around her, and they headed to the beach. My grandma didn't need any *Triple L* app.

I'd been dumped again. I felt like the ugly contestant at a beauty pageant – and not just because the girl across the table was wearing the most gorgeous shimmery red dress with diamond earrings and necklace. She'd painted her finger and toenails to perfectly match her dress. Even her lip gloss sparkled a complementary colour. She didn't look like a computer nerd; she looked like a supermodel.

"The snorkelling is amazing here," I said, in a pathetic attempt at conversation. I wasn't going to let this smart, gorgeous girl think she was better than me. In brains and modelling, she may have had me beat, but I had to be better than her at something. I hoped it was conversation. "Have you been out past the reef?"

"I haven't been snorkelling." She picked up the black leather menu.

"Oh, you've got to go!" I knew something she didn't know. "It's like this awesome different world underwater, and it's right out your back door."

"I haven't had time." She hid behind her menu.

"How about Jet-Skiing? Sailing? Swimming with dolphins?" I listed everything I wanted to do.

"Not yet," she muttered.

"What *do* you like to do?" I said, trying to hide the frustration from my voice.

She peered at me over the top of her menu. "I'm building Ariadne's app."

"You've got to do something for fun."

"Computer games."

I played games sometimes. Maybe we did have something in common. "Which ones?"

"I'm designing one."

Of course you are. I'd had less painful bike crashes. "That's interesting."

"My game will combine action with logic riddles." She lowered her menu and started talking in geek speak about programming and gamer experience and loads of stuff that might as well have been a foreign language. I nodded as if I understood.

Mackenzie flipped the cloth napkin that was fan-folded in front of her and placed it on her lap. I did the same, sending one of my two knives flying. I didn't know what I was supposed to do with that much silverware anyway. My face turned fifty shades of red. Maybe Ariadne could send me to finishing school. They had those in the UK for the royals and posh people, right?

Luke rushed over and picked up my knife. "No worries. I'll get you a clean one." He walked over to a cabinet not far from where we were sitting and retrieved a fresh knife for me.

"Thanks, Luke," I said.

He leaned in closer. "It's nice to see some young people for a change," he said with a smile, took our orders and retreated to the kitchen.

The menu had tons of fish options. I thought of those beautiful fish in the lagoon and decided maybe I was a vegetarian. I ordered vegetable curry because the menu said it was hot and spicy. When it came to food, if I didn't break out in a sweat, it wasn't hot enough. Dad and I emptied a big bottle of Tabasco a month. Mackenzie ordered baked fish. *Blah!* Boiled potatoes. *Bleugh!* And broccoli. *Yuck!*

When I couldn't stand the silence any longer,

I blurted, "What are you really doing here with my grandma?" I cringed. I'd blown my cover story in less than an hour. Ariadne wasn't going to be happy with me. "I mean Ariadne. Miss Sinclair." I corrected my mistake, which only drew more attention to it.

"I knew she was your grandmother," Mackenzie said. "I can see the family resemblance."

"She doesn't like to be called grandma."

"She doesn't seem like a grandma," Mackenzie said. "My grandma doesn't know how to use her iPhone and yours is building apps."

Jealousy zapped me again. She was friends with my grandma. It sort of killed our conversation. Our dinners arrived, and we ate in silence. Sweat dotted my scalp as my tongue burned from the curry. The hot and spicy here was way more hot and spicy that in Indiana.

The sun had set, and the ocean and sky darkened into a black screen. A few red dots blinked in the distance. I pictured sea monsters with glowing eyes. "What are those red dots?" I asked before I remembered I wasn't speaking to her.

"Those are lights from passing ships," Mackenzie said as if she was an expert on everything.

I didn't think the dots looked like they were moving, but I'd have to take her word for it. I didn't love the idea of ships passing out there watching us. I shook off my paranoia. That was my stupid imagination, playing tricks again.

"It was nice to meet you, Charlotte," she said as soon as she'd finished her last bite of fish.

"Chase," I corrected her.

"What?"

"I prefer to be called Chase," I said.

"Oh," she said as if she could not be less interested. "I've got a lot of work to do." She scooted her chair back and walked away.

"Whatever," I muttered and scrapped my chair back from the table. I hadn't finished my curry, but I wasn't about to sit here by myself like some loser while everyone around me chatted, laughed and ate their dinners. I headed for the beach as if that was exactly what I wanted to do.

I didn't need Ariadne, and I certainly didn't need Mackenzie. All I had to do was survive a month of this. I was stuck on a posh desert island, not trapped in a boring old classroom, or tossed in a deep, dark, snake-infested cave. But at this moment, a month felt like a very long time.

6

Dad always said I had a choice. I could choose to be happy or unhappy. He said even at the worst of times there was something to be happy about. Let's see. I wasn't a leper, even though Grandma and Mackenzie had treated me as if I was contagious. I was on a really cool island with no parental supervision. But my life had become an obstacle course and Ariadne, Artie and Mackenzie were massive hurdles.

I woke up the next morning determined to reach happy. The sun blazed through the windows. I blinked at its intensity. The other twin bed was empty, made perfectly without a single wrinkle. I couldn't tell if Ariadne had slept here last night. I found a note on the bathroom mirror:

At yoga studio – A.

I picked up the room phone. "Room service, please," I said when the same lady from yesterday answered. I imagined her trapped in a booth, waiting for someone to call. "Can I have waffles with maple syrup and extra bacon?"

"Yes, ma'am, I'll have your breakfast delivered as soon as it's ready," she said, and hung up. That was more like it.

I wriggled into my swimsuit, which was crusty from the salty ocean water, and threw a T-shirt and shorts over it. I brushed my teeth and combed my hair back into a ponytail. At home I was always on a schedule: Callisthenics at 06:00. Breakfast at 07:00. Leave for school by 07:30. Today I was my own boss, and the freedom felt strange and overwhelming. If I'd been smart, I would have gone snorkelling again or explored the island or built a sand-castle – anything but what I actually decided to do.

Curiosity about my mom was playing on repeat in my brain. Ariadne didn't want to talk about her any more. If I wanted to find out anything about my mom, I was going to have to uncover it somehow. Ariadne had left me alone again, which was practically an invitation to snoop. Big mistake – hers for leaving me alone, and mine for snooping.

I searched every square inch of the room. I wiggled every floorboard and looked behind the abstract smudges they called art hanging on the walls. I discovered my grandma loved clothes. She had outfits of every colour and for every activity – from a hot-pink bikini to a stunning black ballgown. I didn't really need to know that she wore thong underwear. *Eww!* Her jewellery box was messy, but everything else was well organized.

At the bottom of the closet was a safe. I tapped in a few numbers for the heck of it. I didn't know important dates like birthdays or anniversaries or if she had lucky numbers. I gave up and moved on to checking all twenty-three pairs of shoes – usually a good hiding place for top-secret info. I wondered if my mom was as girlie as her mom. I don't know why, but I doubted it.

Then I spotted Grandma's red designer handbag on the hall table. I hesitated. I'd already checked her underwear drawer, why did rifling through her handbag seem a step too far? I carefully unzipped it and poked at the contents. Nothing special. A make-up bag, a pill box, some hand gel, and an orange wallet. No wrappers or lose change rattled at the bottom. My gut told me not to do it, but I couldn't stop now. I wasn't going to steal anything, but I felt like a thief as I opened her oversized wallet.

Several twenty pound notes slotted perfectly in the main compartment. British money was much prettier than America's boring green dollars. Eight credit cards all had their own slots in a panel at the front. At the very back of the wallet was a pocket. My fingers tingled. If I was hiding something super-secret, that's where I'd put it. I slipped my finger inside and carefully removed two sheets of paper. One was a piece of white paper, folded multiple times to fit snuggly into the pocket, and the other was an old photograph wrinkling with age. *Jackpot!*

I studied the three faces staring back at me. One was clearly a much younger Ariadne, and what must be her two teenage daughters. The younger one's ponytailed head was cocked, and she had a goofy grin. I touched the other girl's face, my face. My mom. I couldn't breathe. She was a complete stranger and yet, oh-so familiar. Behind a curtain of straight blonde hair, she had the same look of disgust I had when Dad took a picture of me.

A banging noise startled me. I jumped. The folded paper flicked out of my hand. I snatched for it but ended up swatting it away. It banked off a lampshade and skidded under Ariadne's bed.

More banging. No, it was knocking. Someone was knocking on the door. Guilt shot through me. With shaking hands, I stuffed the photo back where I'd found it and dropped the wallet in her handbag. I exhaled in a whoosh. I'd got away with it. No prison time for me yet.

"Room service," a female voice called through the door.

Almost getting caught made me realize how stupid I'd been. Ariadne wasn't a picture-perfect grandma, not even my idea of a nice person, but what kind of granddaughter ransacks her grandma's room? And what if she'd found me digging around in her handbag? I'm sure her mood would have switched from icy cold to hot anger. She'd probably ship me back on the next slow boat to America.

I opened the door, took my breakfast tray and thanked the young woman who'd brought it. I left it on the desk. Guilt had overwhelmed my hunger. I let the creamy butter congeal in the syrup and the grease dull on the bacon. Maybe Grandma was right not to like me. I had totally violated her privacy. Maybe if I tried to be a better granddaughter, she'd try to be a better granny.

I needed to return that piece of paper to her wallet, zip up her handbag and forget everything I'd learned – especially the thongs. I shimmied under her bed and unwedged the paper from a floorboard near the wall. I crawled back out and stood over her handbag with the folded paper in my hand.

To read or not to read. The angel and demon in my head were arguing. I'd come this far. Why not take a look? It was probably nothing, but it would drive me crazy not to know. On the other hand, it was clearly something private and important. You don't keep random, pointless scraps of paper folded and tucked away. *Argh!*

No, I was going to be good. Even if it killed me. I lifted Ariadne's wallet from her handbag.

"What are you doing?"

I screamed. The voice was coming from the deck. I was caught red-handed. The wallet dropped from my grasp, and this time the paper flicked open a bit as it fell to the floor.

I turned, fighting the urge to raise my hands in surrender as I faced my accuser. Mackenzie stood dripping on my deck in a red, pink, yellow and blue swirled bikini.

"What are *you* doing?" I accused right back. She

had no right to drop in uninvited. Yeah, I'd done it to her yesterday but that was an accident.

"Why are you looking in Ariadne's handbag?" she asked. She wiped away the water from her arms and legs, but she was too wet to come in.

I had to think fast. "I was looking. . ." I peered into Ariadne's bag and spotted her pillbox. "I have a headache and was looking for an aspirin or something." I picked up the wallet and the paper. I sort of accidently flicked the piece of paper by one corner so it unfolded completely. It was a letter. I wanted to study it more, but Mackenzie was glaring at me. She knew I wasn't looking for aspirin. "What are you doing barging into my room?"

"I saw Ariadne at breakfast, and she asked if I'd look in on you." Mackenzie paused and looked down at the water pooling at her feet. "She thought I could download your schoolwork." Dad said he'd arranged for me to keep up with my studies online. I hoped he was joking. Guess not. "I told her I was happy to help."

The girl had an ego that was for sure. "I don't

need your help." But I did need her computer and wifi if I was going to retrieve my homework and online lessons.

She shook her head. Her springy curls splattered water across the floor. "It's not like that. I mean, she asked me to be nice to you."

"How about don't bother?" I said with as much venom as I could manage. I was no one's charity case.

I turned my back on her. It gave me time to check out the letter for a few seconds before I folded it and put it back where I found it.

"I didn't mean it like that—" Mackenzie started.

"Leave me alone," I shouted at her, but I really wanted to shout at my crazy, mixed-up family. I stormed out and slammed the door so hard that the bungalow shook.

I'd noticed three things in the letter before I put it back: the date, the opening line and the logo. Those three clues solved the mystery of my mother. It explained where she was, why she couldn't see me, and why Dad wanted to protect me from her.

The date was from two weeks ago.

The opening line read: *"Sorry to inform you that your daughter Beatrice's parole has been denied."*

The logo was a crown with the words HM Prison Service printed underneath.

Of all the mother–daughter scenarios I'd concocted over the years, I had never ever dreamed that my mom was in prison.

7

As I raced to the office, I had the strange sensation that I was being followed. It was probably my over-active imagination playing tricks on me again. I had more important things to worry about than some senile senior citizen stalking me. MY MOM WAS IN PRISON! I passed the beach and the dining hall. I couldn't shake that *being watched* feeling. When I reached the lobby, I whipped around ready to confront whoever or whatever had me in its sights. No one was there.

"I need to use the phone in Artie's office," I

practically shouted at the receptionist. Artie had the only phone that could reach the outside world, and I had to talk to my dad. I had to know the truth. And the truth couldn't possibly be that my mom was a criminal.

"It's back there," she pointed behind her, "but Artie said no one was to use his office while he was making his rounds this morning."

I shoved passed her. "Sorry, but it's important." I stumbled down a short hall to the only office with a door at the end.

"Wait!" she called. Now I really was being followed. As I reached for Artie's office door handle, she dashed in front of me and blocked the door. She must have seen the desperation on my face. "Oh, OK, but make it quick." She looked around as if we were spies at a top-secret meeting. "He should be back in fifteen minutes. If you get caught, I'll deny everything."

"Fair enough." I slipped inside, pulling the door closed behind me. I dropped into Artie's chair, causing several pages from his desk to flutter to the floor. I picked them up. They were two lists with today's date. One included a numbered list of nearly a hundred names with a special column for titles – Sir, Dame and Lord. It must be the guest list. The other had thirty names on it. I spotted Luke and Artie's names so it must be the staff list. Strange to think there were so few of us stranded on this tiny island together. I placed the papers back on his desk.

His computer screen hadn't switched to standby yet. He must have just stepped away. His email was open on the screen. Red exclamation marks punctuated almost every email message. How could everything be so important?

I dialled Dad's number. As I waited for the call to connect, I took a sneaky peek at my messages. Maybe Shanna had sent the latest gossip. Jacob was going to give me the swim team schedule. I'd even settle for my homework list and class notes from Dana. Nothing but junk. Not a single message from any of my friends. I checked social media as the phone began to ring. No direct messages on there either.

I thought I couldn't feel any worse, but I was wrong about that too. My friends had already forgotten me. I'd always wondered if the only reason we were friends was because we lived in the same small town with not much else to do besides hang out. I guessed I had my answer. We didn't have much in common or some BFF connection.

"Hello?" Dad's voice was a croaky whisper.

"Dad, it's Chase," I said in this hysterical way I did when I'd combined a double espresso with a mega chocolate bar once. Volcanic questions erupted in my brain, but all I could think to say was: "I got here OK."

"Ariadne called me yesterday," he said, his voice beginning to sound more normal.

"Oh."

"Can we talk tomorrow?" he asked. "It's the middle of the night here and I've got to be up early for—"

I interrupted. "No, it can't wait."

"Chase, what is it? What's wrong?" He was wide awake now.

"My mom's in prison," I blurted as if he didn't already know.

Static crackled on the line as I waited for him to say something. I prayed he would deny it.

He sighed. "Ariadne promised she wouldn't tell you."

"She didn't."

"Then how—"

I wasn't about to tell him about my snooping. How I found out was not important. "Were you ever going to tell me?"

"Of course I was going to tell you. Your grandma and I were going to talk to you at the end of your vacation. We agreed it was time for you to know the truth."

"Really?" How was I ever supposed to believe him again? He'd kept this massive secret from me my whole life.

"Chase, you know I love you," he said in that super sensitive way that only dads who have changed your diapers, told you bedtime stories and never ever failed to pick you up from school or missed one of your stupid swim meets or bike races can say.

"I know," I begrudgingly admitted.

"I've never lied to you," he added. "I didn't tell you the entire truth about your mom, but I never lied to you."

Something was slipping away from me. He wasn't who I thought he was, which meant I wasn't who I thought I was either. "Is that why you were always training me? Are you afraid she'll come after me?" Then the worst thought struck me. "Are you afraid I'll turn out like her?"

"No, I wanted you to be able to take care of yourself," he said. "It's what my dad did with me. You were capable and always seemed to like our little training exercises."

"I did," I said, but the truth was I enjoyed spending time with my dad. I would have preferred fewer drills and more plain ol' fun.

He cleared his throat. "Chase, I was scared of losing you. I'm a soldier trained for battle, but nothing prepared me for taking care of a little baby. It was much harder than boot camp."

"Oh," I murmured. So that's what I was, hard work.

"The biggest surprise and the scariest thing was how much I loved you." His voice softened. He didn't talk about feelings very often. "I know I've been overprotective, but it was only because I worry about you."

I was feeling better, but I had to know. "What did she do? Why is she in prison?"

"She made big mistakes and is paying for them," he said, as if he'd been practising that line all my life.

"But Dad—"

"What are you doing in my office?" Artie slammed open his office door. I sprang from his seat. He brushed me out of the way, shuffling the papers on his desk into a pile.

I managed to keep hold of the phone. "I better go," I told Dad. "Can we talk later?"

I didn't hear his answer because Artie ripped the phone out of my hands and hung it up. "You have no right to be in my office." He was red-faced and shouting.

The look in his eyes scared me. "I-I'm sorry," I stammered. "I-I needed to call my dad and let him know I was OK." I backed away and kept right on backing out the door. He continued to bellow about privacy and respect and blah, blah, blah. How could Ariadne like this guy? He tried to appear all Mr Nice Guy but under the surface lurked Mr Nasty. When I reached the lobby, I bolted.

I ran until I reached the ocean. I saw a sign with two arrows: one to the yoga studio and the other to the Aquatic Centre. Ariadne was probably at the yoga studio, and I didn't want to see that mother-of-a-criminal right now. My pace slowed as I weaved down the sandy path towards the Aquatic Centre. I heard footsteps behind me again.

Was Artie following me? He didn't scare me. The worst he could do was send me home. Um, yes, please!

I whipped around. "What do you want?"

But it wasn't Artie.

8

Mackenzie stood there blushing as if I'd caught her snooping in her grandma's handbag. "I wanted to make sure you were OK." Mackenzie said. "You were a little angry earlier."

"I'm fine." I replied. "Are you spying on me?"

"No," she said, but she clearly was.

"What's wrong with you? Yesterday you didn't want anything to do with me, and today you won't you leave me alone."

"I wanted to say sorry about yesterday." She twisted on her tiptoes. She was nervous. It was obvious from her complete and utter lack of eye contact. "I'm better with computers than people, and it's been a long time since I saw someone my age, and there's a lot stuff going on and I was rude and there's no excuse for my appalling behaviour."

I didn't quite know what to say. I wasn't expecting that. "Yeah, I know what you mean." I started walking again. "I've got things going on too and it's ... well, I could have been nicer this morning." I paused and called back to her. "Are you coming?"

She rushed up next to me. We gave each other these forced smiles. Neither of us knew what to say next. It wasn't horrible, just awkward. The Aquatic Centre was up ahead. It was a large glass building with jetties fanning off it. A few rowboats were tied up there, and a Jet Ski was bobbing on the jetty nearest the beach. It was exactly the thing to take my mind off everything. When I needed to think – or not think – I'd ride my bike as fast as my wheels would take me and jump anything that got in my way.

"How about a ride?" I asked Mackenzie. I walked right over to the Jet Ski.

"They won't let us take them out by ourselves," she said.

I checked. It had the key in the ignition. "Then maybe we shouldn't ask." I hopped on the Jet Ski and felt the thrill of the race bubble inside me. "Come on."

She looked around. No one was in sight.

"We'll take it for a quick spin," I said. "No one will know."

"I don't think so," she said, and rubbed the scar on her neck.

"Well, I'm going with or without you," I said, and clipped the key chord to my T-shirt.

"Do you know how to operate one of these?" she asked as she stepped closer.

"Can't be too hard," I said. I'd driven quadrunners on my friend's farm before. I played with the controls until I figured out how to start and drive the thing. "You coming or what?"

"You shouldn't go out by yourself," she said, and climbed on behind me. "I'm only going as a safety precaution." Was she always this much of a goody two-shoes?

"Whatever," I muttered, but I could see a smile twitch at the corners of her mouth. She wasn't doing this for me. She was coming along because she'd been trapped in her room staring at those computers for too long. The girl was in some desperate need of fun. I kicked us away from the jetty. We rocketed out to sea. She shrieked in surprise. Wind whipped my hair straight back while salty spray stung my skin. "Wooooooohooooooo!" I shouted. Mackenzie hugged me tighter as I pushed the machine faster and faster.

If I wasn't so freaked out by my criminal history, I'd have loved this: jetting out to sea with nothing but speed to feed me. My body hummed with the vibration from the engine, but my head rattled with worry.

My mom was a criminal who had made mistakes. Dad clearly said mistakes with an S. I had made MISTAKES too – all capitals and many, many S's – from wrecking my bike jumping the neighbour's pond last year to borrowing and ripping my friend's favourite jeans to redecorating the front hall of our house with a crayon mural when I was five. Maybe Dad wasn't afraid that I'd end up like Mom. But I was. I shared her bad DNA. I punched the accelerator again, attempting to escape these new fears about me and my mom.

As the island faded from sight, I realized I liked having Mackenzie along for the ride – even if she was digging her manicured fingernails into me and screeching in my ear. It might have been a bit scary out here on my own. Mackenzie was shouting something at me, but I couldn't understand over the roar of the engine and the rush of the wind. She was probably saying *slow down*, which I didn't want to do. Speed was the only thing that was keeping me from going crazy.

"Chase! Chase!" she leaned in and shouted directly in my ear. I brushed her back. She pounded her fist on my ribs.

"What?" I glanced at her out of the corner of my eye. She was pointing straight ahead.

I followed her line of sight. We were headed straight for a super-sized yacht. My response was instinctual but stupid. I jerked away from the yacht. Mackenzie and I went flying off the Jet Ski and plunged into the ocean.

I was disoriented but only for a second. I pulled myself towards the light. I was used to wrecking my bike. I knew how to crash-land from years of experience. I assumed the only things rugged about Mackenzie were her credit cards from buying expensive designer clothes. I burst through the surface of the water and spun around and around. "Mackenzie! Mackenzie!"

The yacht was anchored maybe one hundred feet away. The Jet Ski had skidded about the same distance in the opposite direction. Panic zapped me. If we'd hit that big thing at the speed I was going, we'd be scattered like fish food across our little bit of the Indian Ocean.

"Mackenzie!" I flailed in the water, splashing in one direction and then the other. What had I done? No life vest. No helmets. I'd acted recklessly, and

Mackenzie could really be hurt. Could my life skid out of control this easily? Did one mistake like this set my mom on her path to prison? If Mackenzie was really hurt, my grandma would never forgive me, and I'd never forgive myself. *How could I be so stupid?*

"Mackenzie!" I called again, more desperate, more scared.

And then a springy head of curls sprang from the water. Mackenzie spat and spluttered. She was going to be furious with me. She whipped curls away from her face. "That was bloody amazing," she said, and burst out laughing. A smile electrified her face. She looked like a different girl.

I swam over to her. "I'm so sorry."

"Don't be," she said, and splashed me. "I loved it. How did you know how to zigzag and jump waves like that?"

"You know computers, I know bikes." I splashed her back.

"What a feeling! I never knew. We were out there in the middle of nowhere and you zipped here and there—" She was a Coke bottle that had been shaken for ever and then – *wham!* – she was bursting with excitement.

"Yeah, I know, right," I interrupted her stream of conscious babbling. "I've never driven that fast before, and in the water it's like you're flying, and then when we crashed. That was, like . . . wow!"

"Can I drive this time?" She bounced in the water.

"Yeah, sure," I said.

I swam for the Jet Ski while she did his weird doggy paddle, whipping her hair from side to side as if she didn't want to put her face underwater. I reached the Jet Ski first. It wasn't easy to climb back on. I finally scrabbled back on the seat as Mackenzie reached me. I steadied the Jet Ski and helped her on.

"We need to go," she whispered and fumbled with the key. Her smile was gone and she seemed nervous again.

"OK," I said. She was shivering even though it was boiling hot out here.

"Please, Chase," her voice trembled.

"What's wrong?" I asked.

"Someone's watching us." She nodded towards the yacht. "I should never have left the island."

I glanced at the yacht. She was right. Someone was on the top deck with binoculars trained on us. We'd almost rammed their ship so it wasn't so weird that they were checking us out. But I could feel it too; something wasn't right. Maybe it was Mackenzie's reaction or the way the guy kept right on watching us until we zoomed out of sight. Mackenzie drove us straight back to the island at half the speed I'd managed. I thought I spotted a sea turtle passing us.

The only thing worse than some creepy rich guy leering at us was the sight of an absolutely furious Artie and Ariadne when we returned to the Aquatic Centre. I'd been here less than twenty-four hours and I was already in colossal trouble. Maybe I was part criminal after all.

9

My prison had shrunk from Indiana to a small
island to a tiny bungalow. Mackenzie and I were
banished to our rooms for the rest of the day. We
were barred from the Aquatic Centre for life. Artie
ranted and raved about theft and destruction of
property. He lectured on how easy it was to get lost
at sea. On and on he went, laying it on super thick.
I understood that we shouldn't have taken the Jet
Ski, but seriously, he was going over the top. His
face was glowing red. The man might have had a
coronary from one harmless joy ride.

Ariadne didn't say one word. She stood there in a bright green kaftan over her hot pink bikini and shook her head from time to time. I didn't know her well, but she looked extremely disappointed, as if we'd stolen the crown jewels or killed a puppy. When I had the chance to defend myself, I explained that it was all my fault.

"I expected more from you, Mackenzie," was Ariadne's response. Apparently she didn't expect anything from me. She didn't know that I knew her daughter was a criminal. She probably thought I was simply fulfilling my destiny. Like mother, like daughter. Maybe that's why she didn't want anything to do with me.

She walked us back to our bungalows. "I'll have your meals delivered," she told us. "I want you both to think about what you've done. Artie did me a favour and this is how we repay him. What were you thinking?"

I opened my mouth to speak, but she raised her hand to silence me. "No excuses."

The afternoon was agony. I laid out on the deck

pretending not to care that Ariadne was angry. If she wasn't going to talk to me then I wasn't going to talk to her. I was relieved when she changed into a bright yellow dress and left for dinner.

I pounded on the wall I shared with Mackenzie. I felt horrible about dragging her into my craziness. She didn't deserve to be grounded too.

"Go away!" she shouted through the wall.

"I'm really sorry!" I shouted back and pressed my hand on the wood as if I could shove my sincerity through the wall. I thought we'd had fun earlier. There was a glimmer in that moment when I'd thought we might be friends. Not the kind of friends I had at home, who were fun to hang out with, but a real friend with a connection to something that wasn't just the same school or a love of bikes or swimming. What did my dad say about his two Navy buddies, the ones who'd been his best friends for thirty years? *Friends help you move; your best friend will help you move . . . a body.* I had loads of friends, but no partner in crime. And maybe this was the reason. I didn't know how to be the kind of friend that moved bodies either.

"Mackenzie?" I called again.

"Leave me alone!" she shouted back.

Well, that was pretty clear.

I flicked through my graphic novels. Dad had got me hooked on superheroes. Today I wasn't focusing on the heroes. My thoughts kept drifting to the baddies. Was my mom a super-villain like Lex Luthor, Cat Woman or Mystique?

I kept thinking about the few details I knew about her. I remembered the picture hidden in Ariadne's handbag. I looked like my mom. Same hair. Same eyes. Same round face and small nose. I wanted to look at that photo again, but when I came back to the room, Ariadne's handbag was gone. I noticed she had locked her jewellery box in the safe. My own grandma was suspicious of me. You *borrow* one Jet Ski and nearly crash it into a million-dollar yacht and you're the Maldives Most Wanted.

Most wanted. That was funny. I was the most unwanted.

But my mom hadn't deserted me. The fact that

she couldn't have visited me made me feel better. People went to prison for lots of non-scary things. Didn't they categorize crimes as white and blue collar? I wondered if there were also fuchsia, teal, coral and chartreuse crimes. Maybe Mom had committed one of the lesser-colour offenses.

I watched an orangey-pink sun disappear at the horizon. My vacation had gone from awkward to awful. I'd never felt more lost and alone in my life. I wondered if this was what Mom felt like – stranded and lonely with no way to escape.

Escape. Maybe that was my only answer. I checked my watch. It would be early morning in Indiana. Artie and Ariadne would be swooning over dessert about now so I could probably sneak into his office unnoticed, call Dad and tell him I wanted to come home.

I dressed in a pair of cut-off jean shorts and shirt that I tied at my waist. It was the closest I could get to super stealth mode being the only short, blonde, white kid on the island. I decided to stroll along the beach that separated the bungalows and the Aquatic Centre. Everyone would be in the dining hall, so I'd approach the lobby from the back.

The sand warmed my feet as I walked along the shore. Away from the lights of the bungalows, the sky came alive with stars. At home the night sky was dotted with faint stars. Here there were more stars than sky. And not only that, they sparkled brighter, as if my home-grown stars were made of glass and these diamonds. I never knew there were so many stars in the universe.

Something furry brushed my leg and I jumped. It was only a cat. I scratched behind its ears. The night was so quiet that the cat's purring surrounded me.

"You are much better company than that stupid ol' Mackenzie," I told the cat, which made her purr louder.

I wished I could go back to yesterday and start again. I wouldn't snoop or ask too many questions. I was happier thinking my mom could be a fairy princess or simply a donated egg. I would be on my best behaviour and then maybe my grandma wouldn't completely hate me.

My pity party ended with a *bang*.

Actually a series of ear-splitting bangs.

The cat bolted, and I lunged for a nearby palm tree.

Screams erupted from the direction of the dining hall.

Was that gunfire? I'd only heard guns on TV and movies.

I must have imagined it. My stupid imagination was in overdrive. Maybe it was movie night, and they were showing a gangster movie.

More shots. More screaming.

That wasn't a movie. I dived face down into the shrubs.

The island was under attack!

I'd been scared before. When I was four and got lost in a cornfield. That time a snake slithered across my sandals when I went on a nature walk with my Brownie troupe. We had a tornado touch down two blocks from our house, but that wasn't really scary because Dad was with me. He had constructed a cosy and architecturally sound bunker in our basement. He also sang *One Direction* songs badly to distract me when it sounded like a train was passing over our house.

Bang! Bang!

There it was again. The blasts shattered the silence and rippled around the island. I crouched behind a palm tree and squeezed my eyes shut tightly.

More screams.

I wasn't scared; I was terrified. I thought it might be an earthquake until I realized that my body – not the earth below me – was shaking.

The island was deadly quiet. My brain flashed to every horror movie I'd ever watched – zombies, vampires, slashers with butcher knives, clowns with sledge hammers . . . a slideshow of horrors zoomed by in freakish fast-forward.

Think. WWDD. What Would Dad Do? Fear had whipped my mind into a big gooey marshmallow.

Breathe. That's what he told me when I wrecked my bike and broke my wrist. I inhaled and exhaled.

But I was doing it too quickly. My breath was crashing into itself coming and going. *Just breathe*. I calmed my panting into big gulping breaths.

I remembered Dad's advice in case of an intruder: *hide*. We had determined the best hiding places in every room of our house. The best way to survive was to avoid confrontation. I could do that. I opened my eyes. I slithered through the sand and tunnelled further into the mini rainforest that separated the lobby from the beach. I found a cluster of ferns and flowers and burrowed into the sand as deep as I could. I swept leaves and twigs over me. I clawed at the dirt and ground it into my glow-in-the-dark white skin. I smeared it in on my face and muddied my blonde hair. Dad and *Hunger Games* had taught me about camouflage.

And then I waited.

And waited.

For what seemed like hours.

I checked my watch. Only fifteen minutes had passed.

This waiting wasn't easy. Every nanosecond my

brain was making up weird and terrible scenarios. Plain ol' bad guys. Mass murderers. A mutant octopus with a machine-gun for each tentacle. Aliens with blasters that would liquidize human flesh. My body sort of itched and twitched. It wanted to run. I thought of Ariadne, Mackenzie, Luke and Artie. The faces of the old people on the island kept flashing into my mind. I hoped they were hiding too.

My dad told me to hide, but I forgot one important fact: my dad didn't hide. I'd found his Navy medals. I'd seen pictures of him accepting an honour from the President of the United States. If my dad was here – and oh, how I wished he was – he would do something.

Do something.

Do something.

Do something.

I had to do something. But what?

10

What was really going on? I didn't know for sure. And a teeny tiny part of me kept hoping that I'd got it wrong. The island wasn't really under attack. That was insane.

The first step in my stellar *do something* plan had to be gathering information. As hard as waiting was, moving proved to be even harder. I told myself that I was going to stay out of sight and figure out what was happening. That's it.

When I used to be scared or worried, my dad would ask: *what's the worst that could happen?* My answers went something like this: I would fail my math test, which would tank my grade point average, and my low grade point average would mean I couldn't go to college or find a job and Dad would be so disgusted with me that he would disown me and I would end up penniless and dead in the gutter.

Dad promised he would never ever disown me, but he stopped asking about the worst.

What's the worst that could happen?

The short answer was that they would find me and shoot me. But there were simply too many worst things that could happen next – and not just to me. I erased them all from my mind.

I peeked over the floppy, leafy green plants and slowly swivelled. I scanned high and low. No one was around. I strained to hear any sounds. Nothing.

I inched forward, crawling on my belly. I pretended it was one of Dad's obstacle courses. He sometimes used to criss-cross string at knee height up and down our backyard. He'd tie jingle bells to each string then I'd have to make my way to the fence and back without ringing any bells. I never made a sound.

I brushed dried leaves and twigs out of my way so there wasn't a crunch or crack as I moved forward. I stayed hidden in the shrubs while scanning my surroundings.

I crawled until I could see the open-air dining hall. So far so good. I re-camouflaged myself. Slowly I eased up so my eyes were barely above the shrubs. Several masked gunmen were pacing back and forth across the hall. The guests and staff were lying spreadeagle on the floor. I spotted Ariadne's yellow dress. Artie was lying next to her. I ducked back down.

I couldn't deny it any more. This was really happening. Whatever is beyond terrified, that's what I was. Every cell was overwhelmed with it.

"I want wallets, handbags, jewellery and any other valuables on your person." The voice was low and harsh. "My colleague will walk around. Drop your valuables in the bag. Do as we say and no one gets hurt. Don't be a hero."

These were modern-day pirates. They had stormed the island and were looting its treasures. Maybe they would take what they wanted and leave. I found a line of sight through the shrubs. The masked men snatched rings and watches from terrified hostages. They plucked diamond earrings from ears and patted down each person to make sure they weren't hiding anything valuable.

One of the masked men walked straight towards Ariadne. "You!" he barked.

I clapped my hands over my mouth to smother my cry.

Please not her, I silently begged. *Please not my grandma.*

The man pointed his gun at Ariadne. I wanted to look away but I couldn't. Then he shifted his aim, directing it at Artie, who was lying next to her. "You're the manager here, aren't you?" the man shouted.

Artie didn't move.

The gunman kicked Artie's side. Artie flinched.

"Get up!" The man hauled Artie to his feet.

"Please," Artie begged. "You've got what you

came for. Just go."

The man slapped Artie hard across the face. "Shut up!"

The whole island seemed to gasp.

"Shut up! All of you!" The man waved his gun in a wide arc. "You are going to open the safety deposit boxes and the main resort safe. Then we are going to call everyone in one-by-one. You will help me transfer funds from their bank accounts. If you do as you're told, no one will get hurt."

The man led Artie through the dining hall. They were heading my way. I slowly eased down to the ground until I was lying flat. I closed my eyes wanting to believe that if I couldn't see them, they couldn't see me.

"I can't," I heard Artie say. "These people trust me. I won't betray them," he was shouting now, shouting very loudly.

What was he doing?

I heard a scuffle and what I thought were fists hitting bodies. More shouting, but I couldn't make out words, just anger and fear and. . .

Thud!

The unmistakable sound of something hard hitting the ground.

Screams erupted again. My eyelids sprang open.

I stifled a gasp as Artie's lifeless body came into focus.

11

My brain sort of switched off. I couldn't think, couldn't face what had happened. I curled in a tight ball and wished that I could fall asleep and make this go away.

I'd been wrong about Artie. He may not have been the nicest, but standing up to the bad guys was super brave. I was the worst judge of character ever.

"Let that be a lesson to anyone who wants to be a hero," one of the pirates was shouting. "Do as you're told and no one else has to get hurt."

He didn't have to worry about me. I didn't want

to end up like Artie. This wasn't some action movie. The bad guys weren't messing around.

I begged my body not to move, not to twitch. The pirates walked away, dragging Artie between them. I heard a snatch of conversation as they passed only a few feet away.

"We've got to make sure the guests are accounted for."

"I'll check the guest registry and the staff list."

I remembered seeing those lists on Artie's desk. I wasn't on any of them. They wouldn't be looking for me. If I stayed out of sight, maybe I would survive. Then I remembered – I wasn't the only one who wasn't technically supposed to be here. I'd nearly forgotten about Mackenzie. I hoped Artie hadn't included her on any of those official lists either. The pirates might never know we were here. They wouldn't be looking for either of us. We were secret weapons. I liked the sound of that.

"Shut up!" one of the pirates yelled.

My ears were sort of ringing. The sound was

more like static. No, that wasn't right either. It reminded me of crickets on a summer night. Back in Indiana, that sound was my lullaby. I found it comforting to think of those creatures out there making music for me. At home their chirping bounced from field to forest and surrounded me.

But this sound wasn't crickets. It was the sound of people sobbing.

That sound shifted something in me. That's when I decided.

They were helpless. I wasn't. I could stay curled up like a baby and hope and pray that everyone would be OK. I could close my eyes and pretend this wasn't happening. That wouldn't make my dad proud. Or I could be a secret weapon. I was going to find Mackenzie and then together we would figure out a way to get help.

When the coast was clear, I crawled through the jungle, ducking behind palm trees. When I reached the beach, I charted a course from sunlounger to cabana. Four dinghies were lined up on the beach. Those had to be the bad guys.

I searched for pirates and then darted to my next hiding place, until I reached the pier which led to the water bungalows. Tiny twinkle lights lined the elevated walkway. Once I'd climbed up on to the pier, there would be nowhere to hide. Mackenzie's bungalow was at the end. I would have to make a run for it. I would be completely exposed. What other choice did I have?

I wasn't the fastest runner on my best day in track, but I wasn't the worst. I swallowed hard. I had to do it. I bounced to warm up. I'd pretend this was a race.

Every minute I wasted might cost Mackenzie her life. I pictured her sitting in front of those computers with her headphones on unaware of any danger. What was I waiting for?

I scanned the island one last time and then I had to move. There were no pirates in sight.

On your mark... I told myself.

Get set... This was probably the stupidest thing I had ever done.

Go! I bolted down the pier as fast as my legs

would take me. I looked left and right for any signs of the bad guys. The coast was still clear. I might have said the island looked peaceful. But I knew gunmen were lurking in the shadows, and I'd seen what they did to Artie.

I lunged for Mackenzie's bungalow as if it was finish line tape and I was going for a world record. I leaned against the front door and panted.

CRASH!

I froze.

The sound came from behind me. I crouched down and checked out the pier. Two masked men burst out of the first bungalow. They were stuffing things in big duffle bags. My body collapsed to the deck with fear. I didn't know they were in there. I shuddered at the realization of how close I'd come to being caught. I was alive thanks to nothing but luck. I prayed my stupid, dumb, unbelievable luck would hold. While half the bad guys were forcing the hostages to drain their bank accounts, the other half were robbing the guest rooms – and they were heading this way.

I gently eased the door open until there was a Chase-sized gap, and I slipped in. I'd made it. I sighed as I closed the door behind me.

An arm grabbed me from behind, and a hand clapped over my mouth. Terror ripped through me.

"Don't make a sound," a voice whispered in my ear.

12

This was a life or death situation. Those years of training kicked in. I slumped in my attacker's arms. When he loosened his grip, *WHAM!*

One elbow connected with face and the other with ribs. I used the force of the blows to propel me out of his grasp. I whipped around prepared with a wheelhouse kick, but I stopped mid-sweep.

"Mackenzie?" I stared wide-eyed at the girl in silky blue pyjamas who was rubbing her jaw and side.

"Did you have to go all ninja on me?" she said, wiggling her jaw.

"Uh, sorry. I thought you were one of the pirates."

"Pirates?" She looked at me as if I was crazy. "I didn't want you to scream. What's going on? Did I hear gunshots?"

I nodded and suddenly felt vulnerable standing in the bungalow with its two walls of windows. I yanked her to the floor and as quickly as I could, explained everything. Mackenzie listened. She didn't say a word, only touched the scar on her neck and then covered it with her hand. When I'd finished, I gave her a moment. It was a lot to take in.

"Show me how to unlock one of these," I said, pointing to her bank of computers with screens waiting for passwords. "We need help, and we need it now."

"Give me a second," she said, and nervously rubbed her scar. "I need to think."

"Well, think fast because those pirates are headed this way," I said. "I'll send a message to my dad. He works for the Pentagon. He'll know what to do."

"I've got a better idea," Mackenzie said. She

darted to the closet. Inside hidden behind six pairs of sandals was a safe. She punched in a four-digit code, and the safe door popped open. She removed a satellite phone. My dad used them in the military for a secure channel of communication.

"Why do you have a satellite phone?" I asked, and backed away from her. Who was this girl anyway? Why was she hiding out on the island with my grandma?

"My mum is a member of the Royalty Protection Command."

"What?" I exclaimed and then lowered my voice. "Like James Bond?"

"Not exactly," Mackenzie replied. "She protected the royals for a while, but now she does more behind-the-scenes stuff."

Any other time I would have asked a million questions, but not right now. "Call already!"

Mackenzie dialled the phone number and held the phone so I could hear too. "It's ringing."

My insides were riding a killer rollercoaster. Part of that feeling was hope. Maybe we would survive. The other thing that was spiralling out of control in my tummy was jealousy. I always felt a little jealous when other people talked about their moms. Mackenzie was not only a computer genius with a model's body, but she also had a mom she could be proud of.

Mackenzie was looking more worried with every ring. Her mom wasn't answering. We flinched when we heard the pounding of footsteps on the pier. The pirates were getting closer. Then. . .

CRASH!

Mackenzie and I dropped to the floor. I thought the pirates had broken into Mackenzie's bungalow. But the shouting and banging were coming from next door – the bungalow I shared with Ariadne.

"We've got to leave now." I grabbed Mackenzie's wrist and pulled her towards the deck.

"But my mum. . ." Mackenzie started. "I need to leave a message."

I ripped the phone out of her hand and tossed it on the bed. There was no time for that any more. As silently as I could, I opened the sliding door to the deck.

"We're going to have to swim for it," I whispered as we crawled to the ladder.

The sound of the pirates trashing my stuff was making me crazy. I imagined them ripping up my favourite T-shirts and stealing Ariadne's jewellery.

"Climb down the ladder," I explained. "Slip as quietly as you can into the water. Swim to the yellow flags on the reef. Do you know the ones?"

She nodded.

"Swim as far as you can underwater. You can do that, can't you?" I remembered her weird doggy paddle earlier. She nodded again. "Only come up for air when you have to. Let's go!" I stepped half-way down the ladder, but she wasn't following me. What was wrong with her?

I climbed back up. "Mackenzie!" I hissed. "What are you doing? Come on!"

Mackenzie shook her head. She must be more terrified than I was. I silently thanked Dad for preparing me for the worst. I shoved down my panic. Mackenzie needed me to be calm and in control.

"Mackenzie," I whispered in my most soothing voice, "you have to come with me. Right now. We don't have a choice. Follow me. Do what I do. Don't think about anything else but following my lead."

She sat there.

I scrambled on to the deck. "We'll do this together." I crouched behind her and nudged her towards the ladder. "You climb down one side of the ladder, and I'll climb down the other."

She finally moved. We descended the ladder slowly and carefully. "That's it, you're doing great," I told her.

"There's nothing else here!" one of the pirates shouted from next door. "We've got to keep moving and find the—"

CRASH!

That was the sound of Mackenzie's front door being kicked open.

We had to move right-freaking-now. "Dive in. Swim to the yellow flags."

I shoved her, and she did this clumsy jump and vanished under the dark waters. I could see her trail of air bubbles and the ripple of water as she made her way to the reef.

I dived into the water and hoped my splash was masked by the sound of the pirates smashing Mackenzie's computers to smithereens.

13

Swimming underwater at night robbed me of sight and sound. The sand swirled underneath me as I stayed as close to the lagoon floor as I could. Foreign objects flicked my skin, which made me swim faster. I remembered a hunk of coral about halfway between my bungalow and the reef. I hadn't felt it. Did that mean I was swimming off course, or not as close to the reef as I hoped?

My strokes slowed as I struggled to stay submerged. If I was too far off course, I could surface near the beach or by the bungalows. I would be easily spotted and eliminated like some crazy game of Whac-a-Mole. My chest felt like it might collapse from lack of oxygen. I was going to have to risk a gulp of air. I controlled every muscle in my body, and slowly and silently swam to the surface. It took incredible control to keep myself underwater and steady myself in the waves. I wiped the salty water from my eyes. Darkness engulfed me. I was lost.

Stop freaking out, I told myself. I slowed my breath and let my eyes adjust. I circled my arms and kicked my legs to tread water. I glanced skyward. The moon was shining like a ball of glitter. Whenever I was away from home, my dad would tell me to look up at the moon. The same moon that was shining over me was shining over him too. I think he stole that from some Disney movie, but I liked the sentiment. I wished that moon could beam my dad a message.

I was halfway from the bungalows to the reef. I could see the yellow flag fluttering in the night breeze. There was no sign of Mackenzie. I had to believe that she was making her way to the reef too.

I dived deep and blasted forward. It was as if I had left the planet and was zooming in deepest, darkest outer space. I stretched one arm over my head and kicked with all my might. At last I felt it – the reef. I floated to the surface, confident that my head would be camouflaged by the coral jetting above the water.

Still no sign of Mackenzie. She'd had a head start though. Maybe she was already through the gap in the reef. Or maybe...

I wouldn't let myself think it. I concentrated on moving forward. I was nearly there.

When I reached the flag and the reef gave way, I panicked. The reef was the gateway to a bottomless canyon. Yesterday with the sun shining brightly, this bottomless pit gave me the creeps, but the pirates on the island were scarier. I swam through the gap.

"Chase, over here." It was Mackenzie's voice.

I squinted and saw her coral-like curls springing

up and down in the waves. I awkwardly splashed forward as if I'd forgotten my years of swimming lessons and hours of practice on the swim team.

We bobbed in the waves, crashing into each other and the reef. As I rose above the reef, I noticed something out of the corner of my eye. When a wave carried me high, I spotted two men walking along the beach.

I jerked Mackenzie under. "Oi!" she grunted and pushed me away as she surfaced. "Are you trying to drown me?"

"No," I spat back. "I thought those pirates might have seen us."

Mackenzie peered over the reef. "I think they're patrolling the perimeter of the island."

"How long do you think it would take to walk all the way around?"

"Those guys could be back at the boat dock in fifteen minutes at the pace they are walking."

I was glad to be stuck with a girl who had a brain like a computer. My brain clicked and clanked away too. The boat dock. Why didn't I think of it before?

We'd borrowed the Jet Ski from the Aquatic Centre, but I'd seen boats and Jet Skis moored at the boat dock when I arrived.

I swam closer to Mackenzie. "If we can make it to the dock, maybe we can take one of the boats and get help." There were a lot of *ifs* in my plan – if the baddies hadn't sabotaged the boats, if there were any boats left – but it was worth a try.

"OK," Mackenzie said through chattering teeth.

"Are you ready?"

She nodded.

"We can do this, you know?" I said in my pathetic attempt at a pep talk.

We started swimming towards the boat dock. Waves bashed us into the reef. Jagged coral scraped my skin, but we kept moving. The reef ended and a rock wall began. The wall created a walkway two feet above the water and stretched from the lookout point right above our heads to the boat dock. Mackenzie reached for my hand. She squeezed it so hard it hurt. I nearly cried out until I realized she was pointing. We'd taken too long. The two men patrolling the island had returned and were passing the dock. We pressed ourselves against the rock wall, while the waves shoved us into the rocks again and again. We tried to stay as still as we possibly could. With any luck our head-shaped bumps would blend in with the jagged stones. The one thing in our favour was that the pirates had no idea that we were on this old people's paradise.

The pirates were heading straight for us on the wall's walkway. Mackenzie and I clung to each other and the rocks. The stones were slick with seaweed and moss. Waves crashed over our heads. I splashed and spluttered as I drank in air and seawater in equal amounts. The men were passing only a few feet away and a few feet above us.

They didn't appear to notice us. As they reached the lookout point and turned around, I heard fragments of their conversation.

". . .find the princess. . ."

". . .take her off the island. . ."

". . .all be over. . ."

Mackenzie met my gaze. She must have overhead it too. Her fingernails dug into my skin as she squeezed me closer. I'd seen the guest list; some of the guests had titles like Lord, Sir and Dame. One of those wrinkly old ladies must be royalty. This wasn't just a robbery, after all – it was a kidnapping.

14

Something slimy brushed against my leg. I hoped I was imagining things. We had to blend with the waves and rocks for a few minutes more until the pirates reached the boat dock.

There it was again. Something long and thick twisted between my ankles. I stifled a scream.

Twist and Shout.

It was exactly what I wanted to do as I remembered the nasty twin eels that Artie had said patrolled the rocky canals around the island.

Mackenzie stiffened. She must have felt it too.

Hold still, I mouthed to her. We clung to each other. A scream was trapped in my throat from the pressure of the beasts curling around my legs. Mackenzie's lips quivered as the eels and waves battered her. I kept one hand latched on to the rocky wall and caught Mackenzie's hand with the other. I yanked her back to my side. The eels were circling us in a tighter and tighter circle. I wanted to crawl out of my skin each time those creatures touched me. I recalled their pointing snouts and their thick, snake-like bodies.

This wasn't helping!

The men had nearly reached the dock. Mackenzie thrashed in the water. She kicked me as well as the eels. I glared at her and shook my head. She's going to provoke Twist and Shout *and* draw the pirates' attention. Mackenzie calmed down but her eyes bulged with the horribleness of what was happening. It took great concentration to keep still and let the eels twist around our bodies. Finally the men reached the boat dock.

The eels tugged at our feet dragging us down.

Mackenzie slipped from my grasp. We splashed in the water, desperate to find each other. It was no use. Too many forces were pulling us apart. I clutched at the rocks and prayed Mackenzie would be OK. My hands were cold and the rocks slippery. I couldn't hold on.

I gulped in air and made one final lunge at the rocky wall, clawing with both hands. One of the rocks broke free with a *crack*! I hoped the pirates couldn't hear it, but it didn't matter any more. If we didn't do something quickly, the eels were going to drown us.

The weight of the rock in my hands and the squeeze of the eel around my legs plunged me under. I whacked at the eel as I sank deeper into the canyon. The water robbed me of any powerful blows, but I bashed and kicked until at last the eel jerked free.

I dropped the rock and swam up, up, up. I crashed through the water and spluttered and gasped. Panicked I checked to see if the pirates had spotted us. I didn't see them anywhere.

I was free from the eels and pirates, but where was Mackenzie?

I searched for any sign of her. A few feet away Mackenzie's fingertips rippled through the surface of the water. I dived for her. My body hit hers with a hard *thud*. An eel whipped between us. She was battling it as best she could – but she was losing.

I didn't think. I wrapped my hands around the eel and squeezed as hard as I could. The eel was pulling us further and further away from the island, and deeper and deeper underwater. It twisted in my grasp. I fought to keep it at arm's length, but it nipped at my hair and toes when it got the chance. I summoned my strength and with one final yank, I flung the beast free of Mackenzie.

I hooked my arm around her waist and lugged her to the surface. Soon we were gulping air. We spun in a tight circle, alert and scanning the water for any sign of those beasts. We braced for another attack. None came.

We made a break for the rock wall, swimming as fast as we could. I reached the wall first and towed Mackenzie next to me. We bobbed in the surf, catching our breath. I searched the dock, the pier and the island. Not a pirate in sight. My heart refused to believe we were safe. I was sure my pulse was reaching the heart-attack zone.

"I can't believe you did that," Mackenzie whispered between pants. "You risked your life to save me."

I felt a zing of pride. I had done that.

But her words didn't change anything. We were still in danger, stranded in a dark canyon with deadly creatures below. The island was buzzing with men who would kill us if they could find us.

"Why would you do that?" she asked.

"That's a stupid question," I replied. "If I didn't do something, you were going to drown."

Her eyes were brimming with tears. "Thanks," she whispered. She was looking at me differently. Her judginess when we first met, and her anger from this afternoon, were long gone.

"Let's get out of here," I told her. We swam straight for the dock. We wanted out of the water as fast as possible. I was pretty sure I broke my swim-team free-style record as I lifted myself up on to the boat dock. Mackenzie was a minute behind me. I helped her up. We collapsed like a couple of fish destined for the dinner table.

The boat dock was covered with a thatched roof and had a half wall on two sides. There were openings towards the sea and back to the island.

"I can't believe we made it," Mackenzie said when she'd caught her breath.

I shrugged. "I never doubted it." One look at me and she knew I was lying. We burst out laughing, a whispering, snickering laughter. It seemed impossible that we were alive. We should have died like ten times already. Our laughter was uncontrollable and bordered on crying. The more I tried to stop, the more the wild feeling took hold. We rolled on our backs, clapping our hands over our mouths until the feeling drained away.

"I'm sorry I was horrible to you earlier," she said.

"Yeah, and I'm sorry about getting you in trouble." We stared at the ceiling as if the answers to the universe were written there.

"Guess it doesn't matter much now."

Nothing mattered unless we survived. "I think we make a pretty good team," I said. I thought about what my dad had said about best friends helping you move bodies.

She nodded.

Mackenzie raised herself on to all fours and crawled to the edge of the shelter. She peered over the wall and scanned the island. "All's clear."

I checked the sea. Several blobs floated in the distance. The boats and Jet Skis had been set adrift.

"You should go for help," Mackenzie said, crouching down next to me. "That's the way to the closest inhabited island." She pointed out into the darkness. Something had changed in her. She was confident and, well, bossy again. "It's due northeast. There's a resort there. They should be able to send help. The island is approximately ten point two miles away. Based on your inexperience and exhaustion, I'd estimate it might take you twenty minutes on the Jet Ski."

"Yeah," I said, but her math talk was confusing me. We were going to have to swim out to one of those Jet Skis. We needed to head northeast and drive as fast as we could. That is, if I could bring myself to go back in the water. "We can do this," I said, trying to convince myself more than her. She gave me this squint stare as if I was the one confusing her.

"Did you hear what those guys said about a princess?" I asked, stalling. "It sounded like they're planning to kidnap someone. You must know almost everyone on the island. Any idea who they mean?"

"Are you sure that's what they said?" Mackenzie studied the horizon.

"No." I wasn't sure about anything any more. "Is it possible that one of those old ladies is a princess? You're British. You must be able to spot royalty."

I saw a glimmer of recognition in Mackenzie's eyes. "I think royals come to remote islands not to be recognized. One of those ladies could be a princess.

If that's even what you heard. Sounds crazy to me. They could be using princess as a code name." She nervously rubbed the scar on her neck.

Something about Mackenzie's behaviour made me think she was hiding something, but I didn't really know her. Maybe she always acted this weird.

"Take one of the Jet Skis since you already know how to operate it," Mackenzie said. "The average speed of a Jet Ski is fifty miles per hour, but I don't suggest you drive it that fast."

"Wait, why are you telling me this? You're coming too."

She shook her head. "I think our odds of survival are better if we initiate multiple strategies. They will have ransacked my bungalow by now. I can use my satellite phone to call my mum or someone for help."

"That is, if they didn't steal or destroy it."

"Then I might be able to rig something on my computers so I can send an SOS."

"I think we should stay together." I didn't want to do this on my own.

"We've got to divide and conquer."

Who did she think she was? Napoleon?

"I don't want to go back into the water." I was just being honest.

"We can do this," Mackenzie said, using my lame pep talk against me. "We have to do everything in our power to get help, right?"

"I guess."

"Good luck," Mackenzie said, clapping me on the back. She was acting all tough-guy, but her twitching eye and shaking hands told the real story. "I'll see you when this is over."

"Uh, yeah..." This was happening too fast. I wasn't ready for her to go. I didn't know if I could make it to the other island. I didn't know what was out there in the dark, waiting to attack.

"I'm really sorry," she said. "I never meant for anyone to get hurt." She pulled me to my feet.

"What? Wait!" Before I could react, Mackenzie shoved me into the water. She dived straight over my head and swam in the opposite direction...

15

How much could one girl take? I was stranded in creature-infested water in the middle of the night with pirates attacking by land and eels by sea. I was completely and utterly alone, and completely and utterly terrified. I trod water and watched Mackenzie swim her weird doggy paddle away. Her plan made sense, but I didn't have to like it. I'd felt safer with her by my side.

Ahead of me was a curtain of darkness. When I was on the seaplane flying here, I noticed the miles and miles of sea that separated the islands. If

I veered off course, I could be lost at sea for ever –
and what was worse, Ariadne, Mackenzie and
everyone on the island would be at the mercy of
those horrible men.

I channelled my fears and doubts and started to
swim. I didn't have a choice, not really. The pirates
would probably return soon. I kept my head above
water. When I thought about being attacked by eels
and sharks and sea monsters, I swam faster.

When I reached a Jet Ski, I latched on to its
bumper. I was floating nearly parallel with the
dining hall. I hid behind the Jet Ski and floated
along. The lights were blazing in the dining hall.
Guests were tied in clusters to the posts spaced
equally throughout. Ariadne was easy to spot with
her short silvery hair and frilly yellow dress. One
of those other women might be a princess, and
if so, she was in greater danger. I had no way to
warn her.

I was scared and exhausted, but I wasn't tied up
and helpless. I had the chance to do something. They
didn't. I climbed on to the Jet Ski. I pressed myself

flat to the seat and studied the island. My head was exploding with questions. Where were the patrols? Had the men finished ransacking the bungalows? If so, where were they and what were they doing? Were they hunting for a princess? If they heard me, would they come after me? Could they shoot me from this distance? Could they capture me before I reached the other island?

I wasn't the best student, but I had never been at such a loss for answers. If this was Rescue 101, I'd have failed already.

I noticed a few men on top of the dining hall. They were attaching something to each post. I slipped off the Jet Ski and paddled closer, towing it behind me so I was camouflaged by its shadow. I inched closer and closer. I squinted to get a better look.

They were placing things the size of shoeboxes with flickering lights on the roof. That didn't make any sense. Why would they put electronic equipment on the roof of the dining hall – especially when they'd gathered the hostages there?

The answer zapped me like lightning. I knew what they were doing with terrifying certainty...

The pirates had no intention of leaving any witnesses. This wasn't going to end peacefully. Those shoeboxes were BOMBS!

Racing off to another island was no longer an option. Mackenzie had been right. We needed multiple strategies. I hoped Mackenzie had made it to her bungalow and was calling, texting, messaging and sending SOS smoke signals. I had to save Ariadne and the rest of the hostages. Right. Freaking. Now.

I tried to add up the bad guys. Two were ransacking the bungalows. Those could be the same two men who were patrolling the island or the two men planting the bombs. I saw at least two pirates guarding the hostages. Another masked man was ushering someone from the office back to the dining room. There was at least one other person in the office making transactions. The bottom line was ... I was outnumbered.

Then, for once, my brain spat out this perfect thought: I was outnumbered, but together *we* – the staff and guests – outnumbered them. I calculated the safest and quickest way to the dining hall. I couldn't believe I was running towards danger. Sure, I was a bit of daredevil on my bike, but if a stunt went wrong, I broke bones. If this went wrong, I could be dead – and worse yet, others could be killed. I glanced up at the blinking bombs. If I did nothing, the hostages were going to die. I couldn't let that happen.

I swam in the shelter of the Jet Ski for as long as I thought was safe, then I swam underwater to shore. I surfaced exactly where I'd hoped, near the yoga studio. I half swam, half crawled to the water's edge. I was going to have to make a break from the beach to the landscaping around the dining hall. I studied the movement of the pirates. It was a risk no matter when I made a run for it. How was it possible that those people's lives depended on me? ME?!

I quashed every instinct that was telling me to swim away or hide. I could do this. I had to do this. My dad was a hero. Maybe I could be a hero too. But then I remembered the other half of my gene pool. My mom was a criminal, and she got caught. How could two such opposite genes exist in one person? I didn't feel half bad, but maybe I was. I guessed this would be the real test to see if I was more like my mother or my father.

I made a few false starts – darting on to the beach and then seeing one of the pirates looking my way and diving back into the sea. If they spotted me, it was game over.

I picked my moment and dive-bombed the shrubbery and plastered myself to the sandy ground. I waited for any sign that they'd seen me. I slowly lifted my head to check. The scene hadn't changed. This close I could see that the hostages were bound with plastic zip ties. I would need to cut people's wrists free.

On the outskirts of the dining room, not far from where I was, I saw the cabinet where the silverware was kept. I remembered Luke bringing me a clean knife from there after I'd dropped mine. If I was lucky, the knives would be sharp enough to cut through the bands. But how was I going to reach the cabinet without being seen? I needed more than luck. I needed a miracle.

Or a distraction.

A miracle in the shape of a cat sauntered into the dining hall. It wove its way among the hostages. It could help me create a distraction. I searched for something to throw. I dug three pebbles from the sand.

"Sorry," I whispered as I lobbed one pebble at the cat and the other at Ariadne as carefully and softly as I could.

EYEOW! The cat screeched when the pebble hit its back and darted away.

"What was that?" one pirate shouted.

"It's a cat, you idiot!" The other pirate laughed.

As the pair watched the cat, I raised myself above the shrubbery. My pebble must have reached Ariadne because she was alert and looking around. I tossed another pebble. It landed a few feet away from her. She followed its trajectory and locked eyes with me. When we first met, I found it hard

134

to believe that she was sixty-nine years old. She seemed to have aged in only a few hours. I could see every second of those years on her face now.

I pointed to my chest and then to the cabinet and hoped somehow she understood. I wished we'd had years together – not only because we might have developed grandmother–granddaughter telepathy, but also because I was afraid that we might never have the chance.

I dipped back down and kept my eyes glued to Ariadne. Her body slumped forward. She twitched and twitched again. She began to wail.

Oh no! Something was wrong with her. She was an old woman. The stress of this had been too much for her. My grandma was having a heart attack.

I flinched when she cried out in pain.

"Something's wrong with Ariadne," the guy next to her shouted.

Ariadne moaned, "Help me. Please."

Did I just kill my grandma?

16

Why didn't they help her?

The pirates glanced at my grandma but did nothing. The two masked men continued their patrol as if they didn't notice her, lying there, writhing in pain. The other hostages stared, open-mouthed. I couldn't move, shouldn't move. If I got caught, what good would I be to anyone?

The pirates didn't seem to care that my grandma was dying. I guessed it didn't matter to them. They planned to kill everyone in an explosion so they probably figured what was one hostage now more

136

or less. How could a human being care so little for someone else?

I thought of my mom. Was she that heartless?

Ariadne cried out again. The urge to run to her side was overwhelming. I battled my need to stay hidden versus my desire to save my grandma. The pirates continued to patrol the room, ignoring her agonizing screams.

The guy next to Ariadne shouted, "Oi! Can't you see this woman needs medical attention?"

One pirate took a few steps towards Ariadne. He sneered at her as if she was a pile of garbage in a landfill.

Ariadne moaned. Her whole body convulsed.

I hugged myself and crouched tighter into a ball to keep myself from bolting.

A woman miles older than Ariadne piped up. "Aren't you going to help her?"

Then every hostage in the dining hall started shouting at the pirates. Inside I was whooping and hollering too. They would have to help Ariadne. They couldn't afford a revolt. Maybe they also understood that they were outnumbered. Finally both pirates made their way to Ariadne. It was a tiny victory for the good guys.

The bad guys hunched over her. Everyone in the room strained to see what was happening. That was exactly the distraction I needed. I dived for the silverware cabinet and eased open the door. I checked the pirates every few seconds to make sure I hadn't been spotted. I plucked out four sharp knives and closed the door again.

Ariadne screamed louder and louder. Was she trying to cover up the noise I was making? Or was her pain getting worse?

Now for the *really* stupid part of my plan. I crept next to the closest cluster of hostages. A few of them stared at me wide-eyed. They scooted over to make room for me, but their expressions said they thought I was crazy. I shook my head and glared at them. I didn't need them drawing attention to me.

I pinned my arms behind my back so it appeared my wrists had been tied together like everyone else. But I didn't look like everyone else. I was a kid surrounded by old, posh, well-dressed people AND I was soaking wet in shorts and a shirt. I was the easy answer in a game of *Which One of These Things Doesn't Belong*.

OK. Not a perfect plan.

Still, I didn't waste a second. I reached for the hands of the guy next to me. I had to be careful not to move the rest of my body. I placed the blade between his hands and the plastic ties, which wasn't easy to do without looking. I positioned the sharp edge of the knife away from him and against the ribbed plastic. Slowly I began to saw.

"That's all we can do for her," the pirate told the hostages. Ariadne had been untied and was stretched out a few feet from where she'd been sitting. Her head lopped to one side at an awkward angle. The sand on the floor puffed near her nostrils. She was still breathing, still alive.

The pirates patrolled the dining hall again. I kept my head down. The plastic I had been struggling to cut started to give. The guy tugged his hands free. I handed him the knives. He nodded the slightest of nods. He understood. He began to cut the bands of the person next to him.

I wanted to check on Ariadne. I needed another distraction. In hushed whispers and the tiniest of flicks of heads and eyes, word spread around the room. I was amazed at what could be communicated with no more than a glance. A group of hostages at the far corner of the room called to the pirates so those of us who were free could move. Some got more knives while the others slipped to another group of hostages.

I kept my eyes glued to the pirates and sneaked to the hostages right next to Ariadne. She looked so feeble.

Wait.

I blinked and looked at her again. Her eyes opened a crack, and she winked at me. She'd been faking it! I should have known. Her moaning and groaning had been a distraction, and it had worked. Maybe we would make a fine grandmother– granddaughter team someday, after all – if we survived.

"Hey, you!" one of the pirates shouted. I bowed my head. Don't look at him. He stomped over to Ariadne, kicking sand as he went. I froze. "I think the old bat is faking," the pirate said, and he poked his gun in her face.

Ariadne flinched.

"What's going on?" the other pirate called.

The first pirate hauled Ariadne to her feet. "Did you think you could outsmart me, you old fool?"

I'd never forget the smile that crossed Ariadne's lips. She may have been nearly seventy, but in that second, the teenager in her came to life. She cocked her head and said, "I know I can."

Then she kneed him right in the zipper! The pirate doubled over in pain. She did this manoeuvre that connected her elbow and knee with his head. He was down for the count. If that was a yoga move, I was signing up as soon as we got off the island.

Now it was my turn. The other pirate headed straight for Ariadne. He was so intent on reaching her he didn't see me coming. I raised a nearby chair and swung it like a baseball bat. He was the ball and

I was aiming for a home run. Baseball wasn't my sport, but the chair connected with his head with a satisfying crack.

And then the only word that can describe what happened next was mayhem. The hostages that were free raced to help the other hostages. A few of the waiters ran to the office. Others took off towards the beach. We were hunting the bad guys now. Both pirates in the dining hall were stumbling to their feet. I leapt on one pirate's back and Ariadne hopped on the other. I looped my arm around his neck. I gripped my fist to complete the circuit and squeezed with all my might. The man was staggering around and flinging me like a twisted towel in the locker room. I didn't let go until he dropped to his knees and then face-planted in the sand. I kicked his gun away.

I searched for Ariadne. Her pirate was hunched on the floor. She stomped on his hand that was holding the gun. "You don't mess with Sinclair ladies!" she said with a laugh.

Abso-freaking-lutely!

17

Our victory over the baddies bound us together like some bizarre old people's football team, with Ariadne and me as honorary captains. Everyone was celebrating. The dining hall looked like a pep rally. But I knew we were far from safe.

"Um, Ariadne," I started but didn't know how to say it exactly. I needed to tell everyone about the bombs on the roof, but I didn't want to create a panic. I wasn't one hundred per cent sure those were bombs.

Luke raced over to us. "I'll take care of those two." He pointed to the pirates.

"That's good," I said, "But—"

He interrupted. "The other waiters have captured at least two more bad guys. We'll tie them up and lock them in the office. A few of the bad guys may have escaped in boats." We weren't the same people we were yesterday. His smiley nature had turned serious. I, well, I didn't know what I was any more. His friends were already carting the pirates away.

"Well done, Luke," Ariadne said, patting him on the back.

"Uh, Ariadne, Luke..." I started again, but he dashed away before I could get the words out.

"Someone needs to..." Ariadne was explaining how we should organize a search and rescue team.

"Ariadne," I said, but she wasn't paying attention to me. People were starting to gather around her. One word was pulsing in my brain – bomb. I had to tell them. "Excuse me," I tried again, but she brushed me aside as she continued to give orders. I couldn't wait a second longer. "Bomb," I blurted, but no one heard me. "BOMB!" I shouted. That got their attention. Everyone stopped what they were doing. All eyes focused on me. "Everyone out of the dining hall!" I shouted and pointed to the ceiling. "I think the pirates planted bombs on the roof."

People scrambled out of the building, running in every direction. In our mad dash, Ariadne rammed into a table and crashed to the floor.

"Go on!" she demanded. "I'll be right behind you."

I wanted to run and keep on running. My survival instinct was in overdrive. But I wasn't about to leave my grandma. I lurched back to her and held out my hand. "No one messes with the Sinclair ladies," I said.

I lifted her to her feet. She was exhausted and our pace slowed.

"Come on," I told her. "We've got to get as far away from here as we can." I didn't know if the bombs were on a timer or if someone had to trigger them, or maybe they weren't bombs after all. I didn't want to wait around to find out.

We staggered out of the dining hall. I was half dragging, half carrying Ariadne. We stumbled on to the beach as. . .

KABOOM!

The fiery blast was like a giant's hand tossing us skyward and then slamming us back to earth. The force crushed my lungs, and for a terrifying second, I couldn't breathe. When I finally gasped, the air had jagged edges. Fire rained down from the night sky.

I raised my head to search for Ariadne, but even that slight movement was agony. I spotted a lump in the sand a few feet away. That had to be her. We were the last two to leave the dining hall. I attempted to stand but couldn't.

The dining hall was a black mass. Smoked oozed from it over us. Hot sparks peppered my skin. I rolled over and over until I reached Ariadne. Sand gritted every inch of me.

"Ariadne," I said, shaking her gently. She didn't move. Her clothes and hair seemed to be smoking. Ash smouldered on her yellow dress, creating black polka dots. I patted her down, brushing off the fiery embers as quickly as they landed. "Ariadne," I cried. We needed to keep moving. The building was burning. The fire was spreading. I crawled to my knees. I tried to prop her up, but her lifeless body was heavier than I expected. There was no way I could pick her up.

I looked around for someone to help me. The hostages were blackened and bruised from the explosion. They looked like zombies staggering to the sea. I waved to the man I'd freed earlier. "Help," I called weakly.

He rushed back to us and scooped Ariadne up. We stumbled forward, away from the blast.

"You are quite the hero," the man said, when we reached the water's edge.

I didn't feel like it. I shrugged.

"I think everyone escaped and that was down to your quick thinking," he said.

Ariadne began to wriggle in his arms. "Put me down."

"Thanks," I told the guy as he lowered Ariadne

to her feet before rushing off to help others.

A feeling swept over me and took me by surprise. It wasn't love. I didn't know her well enough to love her yet, but it was a deep, warm connection that I hadn't felt for anyone except my dad. I hugged her. Her body stiffened in my arms. I squeezed her tighter but she didn't move.

I relaxed my grip when Ariadne moaned. She might really be hurt. "Are you OK?" I asked. Every inch of me was aching. She was way older than me so she must feel a million times worse. I inspected her from head to toe. "What hurts? Is something broken?"

"I'm fine. Don't treat me like an old woman." She dusted herself off and grimaced with pain.

I wanted to point out the obvious – that she was, in fact, an old woman – but for the first time in my entire life, I didn't blurt the snarky comment in my head.

"Thanks," Ariadne said, patted me on the back, and turned to go. "We need to help the others."

And that's when I lost it.

"Thanks?" I flipped her around to face me. My clothes were smoking from nearly being blown up. "I've travelled halfway around the world and nearly got killed, like, a dozen times trying to save you and all I get is *thanks*?" I huffed. "At least that's something. It's more than you've said to me in the past fourteen years."

Ariadne stared at me as if I was one of those complex math equations with more letters than numbers.

"It's not my fault that Mom's in prison." I was shouting now. "Would it kill you to be nice to me? I mean, we don't know each other, but maybe we could. Why am I being punished for what my mom did? It's not fair!" I crossed my arms and stamped my foot. Yeah, I was acting like a toddler.

"What did you say?" Ariadne asked.

"Yeah, I know my mom's in prison," I spat out the words.

"How?"

The heat of my anger fizzled away a bit when I realized to answer her question was to admit I'd been digging around in her handbag. Not my finest moment. "That doesn't matter. What matters is that you hate me, and I haven't done anything to deserve it. Well, not really."

She tried to hide a smirk, which made my anger flare. "What?" I screamed. She was laughing at me, and it hurt – not as much as nearly drowning and being incinerated – but it felt pretty lousy.

"You have a fire inside you like she did," Ariadne said. "Your mum always knew what she wanted and knew how to get it. She was strong and determined."

"I'm not my mom!" I shouted and stomped again – even though I realized she was sort of giving me a compliment. The rest of the hostages were gathering on the beach. The explosion had ignited tiny fires everywhere. Wisps of smoke swirled around us in the sea air.

"I can see her in your eyes," Ariadne took a step towards me. "You and your mum seem more alive than everyone else. You emit this energy. You almost glow with it."

I shook my head. I wasn't like that, was I?

"You saved my life." She reached up to touch my face, but I flinched. "You saved everyone's life. And you are right. You deserve more than just my thanks."

Then *she* hugged *me*. It was what I had been waiting for, but for some weird reason I didn't feel like hugging back. When you had to beg for it, it lost its meaning.

She pulled away and whispered, "Maybe you'll forgive me someday. I should have reached out to you long ago. I thought you'd be better off without me. I was not a good mother. I assumed I would be an equally bad gra—" She stopped herself.

If she couldn't say the word, how would she ever be a good one? "I think I deserve to know about my mom."

Ariadne nodded and looked anywhere but at me. I waited.

Ariadne wringed her hands. "Soon," she whispered, but I felt that if I let this moment pass, I might never ever get the chance to know the truth about my mom.

I shook my head and planted my feet. "Now."

Ariadne searched the night sky as if the smoke drifting across would form the words she needed to say. She cleared her throat. "Your mum was thrilled when she got pregnant." As she spoke her gaze shifted from the sky to me to the ground and back again. "She promised me she'd settle down. She had been in trouble with the law ever since. . ." Ariadne paused, "for most of her life." I could tell she was censoring the story. "Her promise came too late. Her past caught up with her, and she was convicted and sent to prison." She looked me directly in the eyes when she said the next part. "You were born in prison."

It was as if another bomb exploded inside me. I bent over and clutched my stomach. I was going to throw up.

"Your dad took you almost immediately to the States," Ariadne continued. She paced around me as she spoke. "Your mum was devastated, but she wanted you out of the prison as soon as possible. We agreed that it would be best for you to have a fresh start with no connection to her past."

I had no memories of my mother. I'd always assumed I'd gone to live with Dad when I was very young, but Mom and I never had any time to bond. In a strange way I knew that, I felt that, already.

"She loved you – still loves you – enough to let you have a life without her." Tears sprinkled Ariadne's cheeks. So she did have feelings.

I was born in prison. That thought would not sink in. No matter how many times I repeated it in my head, it smacked me and then bounced off like a big rubber ball. There was only one more thing that I desperately wanted to know and not know. "What did she do?"

Ariadne took a deep breath. "She was convicted of multiple homicides."

Multiple! I couldn't speak. I knew she'd done something pretty horrible. They didn't keep you in prison for fourteen years for shoplifting. Maybe she'd accidently killed someone while saving kittens from a burning building, or shot a bad guy who was robbing a bank.

I wanted to ask about Mom's crimes, but I couldn't make myself say: who did she kill and why did she kill them? *Kill* wasn't a word that I wanted to link to the woman who gave birth to me.

"She was sentenced to life in prison," Ariadne continued. "Her parole was recently denied so she's going to be in there for a little while longer."

I wanted her to stop talking. That was enough information. More than enough. After everything that had happened today, this was the scariest. I thought I wanted to know everything about my mom, but now I wasn't so sure. I was the daughter of a murderer. I was scared of myself and what was in my DNA.

Ariadne opened her arms for a hug. I bolted. I didn't look where I was going; I just wanted to run away from everything as fast as I could.

Smack!

I charged right into someone, nearly knocking us both to the ground. I stumbled backwards but kept myself from falling. Dazed from the impact, I looked up at the guy who was dusting himself off. I recognized his over-gelled hair, his pressed white shirt and khaki trousers. But it couldn't be. Was I hallucinating? Was it a ghost? Maybe the shock of the explosion mixed with the blast of info about my mom had finally caused me to crack.

"Artie?"

18

"I-I ... th-thought you were..." I stuttered. I remembered seeing his lifeless body hit the ground.

Ariadne brushed past me. "Artie!" She hugged him. "I thought you were..."

"No, I'm fine," he said, and kissed Ariadne on the top of her head. "They knocked me unconscious and stuffed me in the office closet. The explosion jolted me awake. What's most important is that you – everyone – is OK."

Then he tilted Ariadne's face to his. *Argh!* I

cringed. He wasn't going to... Yep, he was. Artie kissed my grandma. Love Late in Life.

"Um, guys..." I started, but I didn't want to disturb old-people love.

Was everyone OK? I assumed Mackenzie had made it back to her bungalow, but I didn't know for sure. It was the perfect excuse to get the heck out of here. "I'm going to find Mackenzie and let her know this is all over." Ariadne and Artie's faces were still smushed together. *Yuck!* That was definitely my cue to exit.

"Wait!" Ariadne yelled at me. She took one step and then collapsed on to the sand. Artie swept her up in his arms and carried her over to me. They looked like some weird Disney movie poster: *Cinderella and Prince Charming Anniversary Special: where are they after 50 years?*

"Are you sure it's safe?" Ariadne asked.

"Luke said he and the waiters captured some of the bad guys and the others escaped in boats," I reminded her.

"Yes, but can we be sure?" Ariadne wasn't going to drop this.

"You should stay here. I'll go check on Mackenzie," Artie said, and lowered Ariadne back on to the sand.

"Shouldn't you send for help or search for bad guys or help the injured or something?" Basically anything but bug me.

"She's right," Ariadne said. "I'll corral everyone and help those who have been injured. Artie, you send someone for help. Charlotte, you go and check on—"

"No," he said too forcefully. We looked at him in surprise. "I'll check on Mackenzie. Then I'll send for help. Charlotte, you can help Ariadne." Artie dismissed me. "You need to leave this to the adults."

I hated snakes and snotty cheerleaders, I couldn't stand bullies, and I definitely didn't like anything grape flavoured. But what I hated more than anything in the universe was being underestimated. I wanted to tell him everything this fourteen-year-old had done while he was taking a nap in the closet, but that would have wasted too much time. "I'm going to find Mackenzie."

I stormed off and didn't look back.

My feet pounded the sand and then the wooden planks of the pier. One thought was being hammered into my brain with each step: *my mom is a murderer*. I now understood why Dad had protected me from the truth for so long.

"Mackenzie!" I called when I reached her bungalow. I didn't wait for a reply. I barged in. The door had already been ripped from its hinges. "Mackenzie!" I screamed and skidded to a stop when I saw the state of her room. Fragments of her computers, the satellite phone, her clothes and furniture were all that remained. The moonlight created abstract shadows over the wreckage of Mackenzie's life. It was like stepping into an abstract black and white painting. I spun in a slow circle afraid to move in my bare feet.

I jumped when I heard a sound even though it was as quiet as a tiptoe on carpet. Where was it coming from? I heard it again. This time I was able to pinpoint the noise. It sounded like a sniff, and it was coming from the closet – the perfect hiding place.

What if it was one of the missing pirates? More likely it was my overactive imagination. But I wasn't about to take any chances. I snatched up the desk lamp, which was missing its shade and bulb. I held it high as I flung open the door.

A body toppled out.

Mackenzie's body.

I dropped the lamp and reached for her but she scampered away. She was sobbing.

"Mackenzie," I whispered and slowly closed the distance between us. "It's me. It's Chase. Are you OK?" What a stupid thing to say! She obviously wasn't. "You're safe now."

"Everything's ruined..." she muttered, indicating the fragments of her technology. "I tried ... I couldn't ... then ... the explosion?"

"Everyone made it out," I said as I helped her to her feet.

"I thought you were..."

"Everyone's fine."

"So it's over?" she asked.

"Yeah." We hugged for I don't know how long.

It's the kind of hug I'd wanted from Ariadne. Then I remembered. "Why did you leave me at the boat dock?"

I tried to pull away but she held me tighter. "I thought I could call for help or get my computers working."

I ripped myself free. "That's a lie." I'd been lied to enough. It was written all over her face. She wasn't telling me everything. "You said you were sorry, as if it was your fault. What did you mean?" She had conveniently run away and was safe in her bungalow when the bombs exploded. "You aren't working with the pirates, are you?"

"You've got it wrong." She backed up. "I thought they were after me."

"What? Why?"

My question was answered not by Mackenzie but by a masked man as he charged up the ladder and on to the deck. He shoved me aside. I crashed into the closet. Pain radiated from every point of impact. I collapsed on to the floor. I was dazed and couldn't make sense of what was happening. The man didn't hesitate – he went straight for Mackenzie. She dashed on to the deck, but there was nowhere to run. The man lifted her off her feet as if she were weightless. She flailed her arms and legs like a turtle flipped on its shell. She was whacking the bad guy and screaming at the top of her lungs.

I stumbled to my feet and charged at the man, fists flying. My blows bounced off his muscles. I ran at him, then landed a kick right in the middle of his back, which gave Mackenzie the opportunity she needed. She broke free and staggered back inside. I swept her behind me.

The man glared at us. Mackenzie and I were pumped up and ready to fight but the man stood there and laughed. I lunged to shut the sliding-glass deck door that separated us. I fumbled with the lock. "Run!" I screamed at Mackenzie. She bolted towards the front door with me at her heels.

She screamed when she realized the door was being blocked by another masked man.

CRASH!

The deck door shattered behind us. We were

trapped. Mackenzie and I stood back-to-back, ready to put up the fight of our lives.

"Mackenzie," the masked man from the deck said, "you are coming with us."

How did they know her name?

"I don't want to hurt two girls, but I will," the other man echoed from behind me.

I clutched Mackenzie's hand. "I'm not letting them take you," I told her.

She squeezed back.

Both men walked towards us. I punched and kicked as hard as I could, and Mackenzie was doing the same. But these guys had muscles as big as my head. They brushed our attacks aside. One scooped me up and pinned my arms to my side. I wriggled, elbowed and kicked, but he held me fast. The other guy lifted Mackenzie as if she was a bride and he was going to carry her across the threshold.

"We are taking Mackenzie and there's nothing you can do to stop us," my captor barked at me.

A sob burst from my lips. I was so angry.

"Mackenzie!" I called. She locked eyes with me. I've never ever seen anyone so terrified in my life. I shrieked in complete and utter frustration. I tried to think of something, anything I could do, but we were overpowered.

I watched in horror as the man tossed her off the deck. My screams were drowned out by the splash of her body into the lagoon.

19

"Stop fighting," the masked man whispered in my ear. "Or I will end you."

He struggled to keep hold of me as I squirmed in his grasp. The man who had thrown Mackenzie off the deck calmly walked down the ladder. My captor dumped me on to the floor. The shattered glass from the door and Mackenzie's computers ground into my skin. I ignored the hundreds of cuts and scrapes as I rolled to all fours, determined to go after Mackenzie.

He kicked me in the ribs. "Stay down." I crumpled

to the floor in agony.

As he disappeared down the ladder, I heard an engine roar to life. I crawled through the broken glass to the deck's edge. I stifled a gasp.

Two masked men were huddled in the dinghy below me. Mackenzie's body bobbed face down a few feet away. Was she *dead*? She couldn't be dead.

A fight broke out in the boat. The men were shouting. One even threw a punch.

"We can't leave her here like that," one man screamed and manoeuvred the boat closer to Mackenzie.

"What does it matter?" the other guy yelled. Was he going to watch her drown?

"I'm not killing a kid," the guy said as he dragged Mackenzie into the boat.

With every passing second, my panic multiplied until I saw her swing wide and bash one of the pirates in the face. She was putting up one heck of a fight. I'm pretty sure I'd taught her that. As the dinghy zipped away, the other pirate seized her by the hair and shoved her to the bottom of the boat. They may not want to kill her, but they sure didn't mind hurting her.

As Mackenzie's dinghy skidded over the reef, I spotted the flashing red lights of another dinghy waiting outside the lagoon. Both boats whipped out to the open sea. The bad guys were getting away, and they were taking Mackenzie with them.

I didn't think. I raced out of the bungalow towards the island. I had to do something to save Mackenzie. I kept my eye on the vanishing boats. From my vantage point on the elevated pier, I spotted two of the pirates' dinghies banked on the beach. I hurdled over anything in my way.

It didn't matter that it was me against at least four bad guys. I didn't have a clue what I would do when I caught up to them. I would think of something. I was part soldier and part criminal, after all.

I ran to one of the remaining dinghies and pushed it into the water. Every muscle in my body hurt, but I wasn't going to let anything stop me. I leapt in. The dinghy skidded forward. A sharp and swift tug on the pull cord and the engine roared to life.

I scanned the horizon. A cluster of tiny red lights twinkled up ahead. That had to be the bad guys. The light grew dimmer by the second. I jetted off after them.

I cut the motor when the dinghies' red dots slowed and clustered. I floated forward on the momentum of the chase. My eyes adjusted to the moonlight. The outline of a huge luxury yacht took shape – the same yacht Mackenzie and I had nearly rammed with a Jet Ski. If only I'd known then what the guy with the binoculars was planning. . . It wasn't the first time I'd wished for a time machine.

I used the oars that were snapped to the boat to slow myself. I couldn't risk getting too close. The dinghies were anchored to the back deck of the yacht. A Mackenzie-sized shape was being forced up the stairs that lead to the main deck. It took three of the four men to carry the squirming, shouting girl away. The other baddie disappeared on to the yacht.

I watched and listened. I was sure the baddies would make a swift escape. They had their money and a hostage. Why would they stick around? But the yacht didn't move. Then someone must have pulled the master switch because the ship's lights came on. There were running lights dotted around the boat as well as lights in the portholes. A spotlight illuminated the ship's name: *King's Ransom*. If I got within twenty feet of the boat, I would be spotted.

I waited, hand on the pull cord, ready to follow the yacht. Nothing happened. I could see dark figures cross the windows on the upper deck, but the yacht was quiet.

The longer I waited, the more horrible images popped into my brain. They were of Mackenzie and the terrible things they could be doing to her. Maybe they'd discovered she was a geeky genius and wanted her help with techy stuff? If they found out she was the daughter of an officer in the Royalty Protection Command, maybe they would torture her for information? I couldn't sit here any longer.

I floated closer, ducking as low as I could while still being able to row with the oars. I felt as if the rest of the world had vanished, and all that remained was me, four bad guys and Mackenzie. I scanned each deck as I drew closer.

Think like a bad guy, I told myself. My mom was a criminal. Her blood ran through my veins. I'd pretend I was a thief. I was going to have to sneak on to the yacht. What did thieves in the old movies always say – *case the joint*? I needed to figure out the layout of the ship. I counted four floors – one at sea level, two decks that stretched the length of the yacht, and a smaller level at the top. My best shot of helping Mackenzie was if they dumped her in some room and forgot about her. If someone was guarding her, all I had to defeat him with was the element of surprise. Not as good as a gun or a Taser or even a big stick.

I made myself very small as my boat shot into the circle of light surrounding the yacht. Something moved on the upper deck. I flattened myself to the bottom of the boat. There it was again. I wrenched the oars back to stop my forward motion. Shadows flickered on one of the middle decks. Had someone seen me? I slowly began to row in reverse. My eyes ached to blink, but I had to stay vigilant. Maybe they hadn't spotted me. I stopped and bobbed on the surf.

A nasty stench crashed over me. Fish! Not the kind Dad made with garlic and lemon. This was that gross smell of fish guts. Dad and I went fishing, but I never ever cleaned the fish we caught. I hated the smell of fish innards. The smell overwhelmed me as something splashed into the water near the yacht. Two men were on the top deck tossing buckets of something overboard. Were they dumping evidence?

I studied the men and the waterfall of gunk splashing into the ocean. I was so busy focusing on the yacht that I didn't notice my boat drifting back into the light. *Oh no!* I collapsed on to the floor of the boat, covering my head with my hands in a lame attempt to hide. I sneaked a quick look.

Both men were staring right at me. I leapt back

into the seat and fumbled for the pull cord. The engine wouldn't start. I kept my eyes glued to the men. Something in one of their hands flashed in the moonlight. The man was holding a knife. The glare of his smile matched the glimmer of the light on the blade. He whipped his arm back. The knife spun through the air. It was heading straight for me. I ducked.

The knife stabbed the inflatable boat. Air whooshed out making a loud raspberry sound. I opened my eyes. Another knife whipped through the air. I sprang to the other side as it dug into the boat only inches from my head.

I glanced up at the yacht, expecting to dodge another knife or bullets or rocks, but the two men were gone. I didn't understand. Why didn't they finish me off? I counted my blessings, but only for a second. Water gushed over the deflating sides. My dinghy was sinking. I tried to balance on what was now an oversized surfboard, but it was no use. The air hissed out and rocked me back and forth. I toppled over. My feet tangled with the rope, oars and floppy sides. I pushed myself away, afraid I'd be dragged down with the dinghy. I kicked at the boat's debris until I was clear of the wreckage.

I trod water. If I swam to the boat, they would capture me for sure. No element of surprise. No hope of saving Mackenzie or myself. There was no way I could swim back to the island. I was as good as dead.

I didn't want to drown. I took one strong stroke towards the yacht. My hand struck something and then something else knocked into my side. The rancid raw fish smell overwhelmed me again. Bits pinged against my arms and chest. I had floated into the slick of blood and fish bits that the bad guys had tossed into the water. I gagged and choked back the bile rising in my throat. I was coated in fish guts.

I screamed not only because I was the centre of a disgusting sushi roll but also because I sensed movement below me. Then I saw it – a fin cutting through the water. It wasn't the frolicking fin of a dolphin this time.

SHARK!!!

No, not just one shark. I could feel the water boiling below me.

Terror crackled through my body in a way I had never felt before. My body went limp, and I was pretty sure in that second my heart stopped beating. The bad guys weren't going to stab or drown or shoot me. They'd thought of something much worse. They were going to let the sharks kill the kid.

20

Everything came into sharp focus. I aimed myself like a bullet at the ship. With each stroke of my arms and flick of my legs, I imagined the jagged jaws of the creatures chasing me. I swam faster. My hand whacked the deck and groped for something I could hold on to. My fingers curled around the rope that was securing one of the dinghies to the deck.

I shouldn't have done it, but I couldn't help it. I made the supreme mistake of looking behind me. The fin was as big as a bicycle tyre and closing fast. My insides were melting. I summoned every ounce of strength and flung my other arm on to the deck. I wrapped the ropes around my wrists and pulled with all my might. I raked my body over the edge and flopped on the deck. As I flicked my hair out of my eyes, I saw the shark's nose rise from the water. Only inches away from me, its monstrous jaws closed around the bait. That could have been me.

I stifled a sob. I was afraid that if I started crying, I'd never stop. I rolled until I smacked the back of the yacht, which was only a few feet from the edge. More sharks joined the feeding frenzy. I counted at least five. Any one of them could easily chomp the little deck and me in one gulp – a Chase Armstrong pizza.

I scrambled up the stairs. I stopped before I reached the top, slowly raising myself so I was eye-level with the deck. I waited and watched. When I was convinced no one was coming, I crouched down on the deck. I recalled the many times Dad and I played paintball with his Navy buddies and their sons. I was always the only girl on the field – and, according to my dad, one of the best players. He taught me how to assess threats and be strategic with my ammo. Most guys' strategy was *run and gun*, but that's usually not what won the game. *Thoughtful and calculated risks*. We'd lie in wait and pick off our opponents one by one.

I scanned the ship again. I tiptoed to one side and peered around the corner. The coast was clear. I found the stairs and climbed up. I checked left and then right before I crawled on to the deck. I felt far enough away from the sharks. The absolute terror from only moments ago still singed my insides. I was no use to Mackenzie or anyone in this state. I needed to find a place to hide so I could calm down and figure out my next move. There were at least four men on the ship who had already proved that they would do whatever it took to stop me. Anyone who could use a teen girl as shark bait was pretty much capable of anything.

At the back of the ship, I spotted a bar area with leather and chrome stools lined up neatly in a row.

I would have been impressed with this gorgeous yacht – if I didn't think I might die here. I slipped behind the counter and collapsed on to the floor, hugging my knees to my chest.

Except for his little training exercises, my dad had always made sure my life was lacking any excitement and absolutely any danger. Today I'd had enough action for a lifetime and my adventure wasn't over yet. I hated to admit that part of me – the part beat up, blown up and nearly devoured by a shark – wanted to hide out here. Maybe they would never find me. Maybe I could sneak off when they docked somewhere – and they'd have to dock somewhere, wouldn't they? But that was a coward's way out.

Just when I thought I might regain my sanity, I heard footsteps. It was only one person and they were walking agonizingly slowly. I tucked myself under the counter and merged with the shadows. The footsteps stopped. I calculated that the man was probably only a few feet away. I glanced up at the glass case behind me. I rose as high as I dared to see his reflection. He was peering over the railing into the shark-infested waters. Was he checking to see if the pesky girl was floating face down and being nibbled by sharks?

All I had was the element of surprise. I had to act first before he saw me. I sprang from my hiding place and rammed him hard from behind. The force of my attack shocked and unbalanced him. He flew over the railing. I grabbed for him, but my fingers found only air. I hadn't meant to send him over the edge. He screamed as his body splashed into the water. I dived back behind the bar and crouched down. I couldn't think about him in that water. "I'm so sorry," I murmured over and over. *It was him or me*, I told myself. He hadn't cared when he'd made me shark bait. Mixed with my guilt was a tiny dark part of my mind saying, *one down, three more to go.*

More footsteps. This time the baddie was running and calling for Kyle. I didn't want to know the name of the guy I'd fed to the sharks. The man stopped in front of the bar. I checked his reflection. He bowed over the railing shouting for his friend. I picked up one of the bar stools. The sound of the chair scraping the deck made the man turn, but I had the jump on him. I levelled the stool at his head. The impact caused us to jolt backwards. He stumbled into the railing and bounced back towards me.

"You!" he spat.

I raised the stool high. He charged at me as I let it drop. The blow landed on his back. He collapsed to the deck, but only for a second. He hauled himself up. Adrenaline flooded through me. I didn't hesitate, hitting him again and again. With each blow, the guy sank lower and lower until he was huddled at my feet.

He stopped fighting.

I stopped hitting.

A weird calmness came over me. *Think like a criminal, like my mom*, I told myself. Maybe these criminal instincts could save me and Mackenzie.

I rushed down to the lower deck and stole some rope from one of the dinghies. I had to work quickly before the guy came around. I dragged him behind the bar that had been my hiding place. I looked for a gag and found a hand towel, which I stuffed into his mouth, and tied him up good and tight. I knew about knots. He wasn't going anywhere.

Two down!

21

My odds were definitely improving. If I was right, the ship was virtually empty: just two conscious baddies, Mackenzie and me. I was on the move. I bobbed slowly and carefully at each window to see what was inside. This was like a floating penthouse – or how I imagined a penthouse would be. Everything gleamed, from the crystal chandeliers to the marble floors. It sure beat my dumpy, zillion-year-old house. If I survived, my new life's goal would be to have a yacht like this one day – minus the thieves, kidnappers and would-be murderers, of course.

The yacht was eerily silent. I found the staircase to the top level and scampered up. I checked left and then right. No one was in sight. I figured the bridge – where the captain controlled the ship – must be at the front. The ship wasn't moving, but I bet at least one of the bad guys would be there. The only light on this level came from the final window up ahead.

"Shut up!" a man barked. "Stop crying!"

He had to be talking to Mackenzie. I ever so slowly inched towards the lit window and peeked through the corner. Mackenzie was slumped on the floor, her wrists and ankles bound. Her eyes were red and her face was streaked with tears. The final two pirates weren't wearing ski masks any more. That was a bad sign. They didn't care if Mackenzie could identify them.

They didn't look like monsters. The one with the moustache was my dad's age. The other guy was younger and smaller. He had longish hair. Neither one had any tattoos or scars. They looked like normal, everyday guys I might see in the frozen food section of the grocery store. I wondered what had made them bad. Were their mothers in prison, or were they school teachers or doctors?

"Let's get it over with. Kill the kid and dump her with her little girlfriend," the moustached man said.

I dropped to the deck. He talked about killing Mackenzie so casually, as if he was suggesting "let's go to McDonalds".

"I think we should demand a ransom," the other guy said. "I bet we could make more money than they are paying us. She's got to be worth more alive than dead."

"This wasn't a kidnapping and you know it."

I decided the guy speaking was the super-mean baddie and the other guy was just plain bad. "We got half of our money. Now we have to earn it. They won't pay the other half until we finish the job."

"Things haven't gone exactly as they were supposed to," Plain Bad said. "I wasn't supposed to have to kill anyone. The bombs weren't me either. I was hired to rob bungalows and guard hostages –

that's all. I'm not doing anything to the kid until we hear from the boss – and neither are you."

It sounded like they were saying they were paid to kill Mackenzie. That didn't make any sense. Who would want to kill nerdy ol' Mackenzie? And they weren't the masterminds; there was a super-duper bad guy somewhere who had planned everything and had paid these guys to execute his plan.

I'd heard enough. I tiptoed backwards as Super Bad spoke. "I think—"

"Wait," Plain Bad interrupted. "Did you hear something?"

The silence that followed nearly suffocated me. If they stepped into the corridor, I'd be caught.

"I don't hear anything," Super Bad said. "You need to calm down. You are making me jumpy. Find Razen and Kyle and let's get out of here."

"Don't tell me what to do!" Plain Bad shouted.

While they continued to argue, I bolted to the back of the ship. I shoved open the sliding door that led to the massive living room. I needed to hide, but I also needed to find something to use as a weapon. The room was smooth and shiny with nothing laying around, except four furry blue throw pillows on a cream leather couch. This wasn't going to be a pillow fight. I squeezed behind the couch and the far wall. The yacht roared to life.

I heard clunky steps pass by. That must be Plain Bad. At first his steps were slow, but his pace increased until he was running up and down the decks, calling for Razen and Kyle. "They aren't here!" he shouted up to the bridge.

"They've got to be," Super Bad's voice echoed over the ship's intercom. I jumped in surprise. "Check the dinghies."

"I did. All of them are tied to the back," Plain Bad yelled. "Razen and Kyle are gone!" The lights in the room where I was hiding flicked on. "I can't find them anywhere." He was in the room with me. I shrunk as far down into the plush carpet as I could. He kicked at the glass coffee table and mumbled, "Maybe I should take one of those boats and disappear too."

"Get back to the bridge!" Super Bad yelled so loudly I could hear his voice over the intercom and from the bridge. Plain Bad turned off the lights and left.

When I was sure Plain Bad was long gone, I slipped out of the room. I needed a weapon to have any chance of defeating these guys who were about three times my size. I sneaked down to the deck below. There had to be a kitchen around here somewhere, and kitchens have knives. I had been super stealthy, slinking soundlessly about the ship. Now I was bolder because I knew for a fact one baddie was shark bait, one was tied up and Plain and Super Bad were on the bridge. I walked down the corridors like an invited guest.

The intercom crackled to life. "Charlotte Armstrong!"

I froze.

"We know you're here. You need to come to the bridge at the front of the ship. Or else we'll kill Mackenzie."

How did they know I was here? Was there

another baddie on the ship? Had Plain Bad spotted me earlier? Then I saw it. I was looking for people and weapons when I should have been looking for cameras. Up in the back corner of the ship, there was a surveillance camera pointing right at me.

I raced down the hall and dived into one of the many bedrooms. I hoped they didn't have cameras in here. I yanked open drawers and closets, looking for something anything that I could use to defend myself. Empty. Nothing. Zip. Zilch!

"There's no place to hide, Charlotte," Super Bad's voice was everywhere.

How did he know my name? I didn't think Mackenzie would have told them, but I didn't know for sure. If they had threatened her, how easily would she crack under pressure?

"Move! Now!" Super Bad bellowed. The anger in his voice sent a shiver through my body. I forced one foot forward, and then the other. What else could I do? If I did as they instructed, wouldn't they kill us both? If I didn't, they would definitely kill Mackenzie.

I walked back into the corridor and stepped right in front of the camera. I glared into the lens and raised my hands in surrender.

22

I hated myself for being so stupid and getting caught – like mother, like daughter – but I wasn't going to let them see any weakness. Right before I reached the door to the bridge, I paused. I pulled my shoulders back. I walked on to the bridge with my head and arms held high.

As I took in the scene, my confidence drained like the remains of bubble bath in a cold tub. Mackenzie was slumped against the back wall. Her wrists and ankles were tied. Plain Bad had a gun pressed against her temple. Super Bad sat in the swivelling captain's chair in the middle of the bridge, his gun pointed at my head. Mackenzie looked shattered. I couldn't imagine what she'd been through. I tried to smile but my lips twitched nervously.

"Why don't you let us go?" I said, trying to make my voice sound younger and more vulnerable. There was the slimmest of chances that I could convince – OK, beg – them to let us go. "We aren't any good to you. We'll give you plenty of time to escape. No one will ever catch you. How can you murder two young, innocent girls?" I was laying it on really thick. If they had any compassion, they would agree with me. "Why not take your money and run? We are just kids."

If anyone else had said that, I'd be furious. No one my age was *just* a kid. That always made it sound like we were less than people. But I was going to use every trick I could to stay alive.

"Maybe we should," Plain Bad said, lowering his weapon. "The kid's right. I'm a thief, not a murderer."

Super Bad laughed. "Just kids? You risked

your life and you don't even know who your BFF really is."

"What?" I blurted. He was trying to confuse me.

Super Bad pointed his gun at Mackenzie. "Do you want to tell your little friend or should I?"

Mackenzie shook her head.

"It is my pleasure to introduce to you Her Royal Highness Princess Mackenzie Wettin Clifford, illegitimate daughter of Prince Arthur." Super Bad bowed to Mackenzie.

WHAT!!!???

I was speechless. Geeky Mackenzie was the princess they were looking for. It all made sense now. Her hiding out. Her paranoia. I didn't know much about the British monarchy. I'd seen Prince Arthur, his wife and young son on the TV and in magazines. I understood that Prince Arthur would be king one day. Did that mean Mackenzie was in line for the throne?

Mackenzie met my gaze and gave this apologetic shrug. It might have been good to know her deep, dark secret when we were being attacked.

Super Bad shoved me down. I stumbled closer to Mackenzie.

"Sit still and shut up," Super Bad shouted at us. "Watch them," he told Plain Bad. "I know a few guys on another island who might be willing to take Charlotte in trade for another boat. This yacht is too big and too conspicuous." He twisted and turned dials and punched at buttons on the control panel.

I hated being called Charlotte, but I hated the thought of being traded like a rusty ol' used car even more.

Mackenzie finally looked at me. *Sorry*, she mouthed.

I understood why she'd deserted me on the dock. She knew she was the target, and she was protecting me. None of this was her fault. I gritted my teeth to squash the sob that was gathering in my chest. I would not let Mackenzie or these men see me cry. I took one deep breath and then another to shake off the sadness. I had to dig deeper than I ever had before and find a massive, buried-treasure-chest of courage. I half smiled. I hoped she'd see that I'd forgiven her for everything.

The further this yacht got from our island, the better the chance that Mackenzie and I would be sailing into the sunset, never to be seen again. I couldn't believe that not so long ago I was worried that I'd be bored to death. Now death by boredom sounded pretty good to me.

I wanted to somehow communicate to Mackenzie that we were going to put up a fight. Dad said violence was always the last resort. I was out of options. Plain Bad's eyes flicked from Mackenzie to me. Sweat dotted his forehead. He was nervous. He didn't want to do this. He was the weak link. If we overpowered Super Bad, Plain Bad might give up.

Super Bad checked and re-checked readings on the control panel. "Almost ready to go." He pointed his gun at us. "I'll watch these two while you do the final prep of the yacht."

"Yeah, sure." Plain Bad scuttled away like one of those bottom-feeding sea creatures I'd spotted while snorkelling. I could tell he was relieved not to be guarding us any more. They hadn't expected to have only two men to operate this ginormous ship. And they had to do it while keeping guard over us.

Something on the control panel bleeped and distracted Super Bad. This was my chance. One man and one gun. Those were the best odds I'd had all day.

I winked at Mackenzie. That's the only signal I had time to give before I leapt into action. I lunged for Super Bad. Despite being tied up, Mackenzie still did the same only a beat behind. Super Bad wasn't expecting an attack. For once underestimating two young girls had worked in our favour.

I smashed his nose with an upward palm strike – the way Dad had taught me in one of his many self-defence lectures. I threw the whole weight of my body behind it. His nose crunched under my hand, and his eyes flooded with tears as blood gushed down his face. He screeched in pain. Mackenzie charged head first into his gut. He stumbled backwards. With a sweeping kick, I knocked the gun out of his hand. It skittered across the bridge and on to the deck. All eyes followed the gun.

I landed another kick in Super Bad's chest. He collapsed forward so I kicked him again right under the chin. I expected Mackenzie to go for the gun, but instead she hopped to the control panel and punched a button.

An alarm sounded and the doors on either side of the bridge slammed shut. We were trapped in here with Super Bad, but his gun was out there. I kicked him in the gut again and when he bowed in pain, I jammed my elbow in his back. He fell to his knees.

"Watch out!" Mackenzie yelled.

I didn't think; I dived out of the way.

Mackenzie was clutching a fire extinguisher, which wasn't easy with her wrists still bound. She swung it wildly.

Clunk! The metal container collided with Super Bad's head. He wibbled one way and then wobbled the other. He was like one of those clown punching bags that no matter how hard you walloped it, it always sprang back up. Blood was streaming down his face from his nose and the new red knot on his head. I pushed him and that was all it took to send him crashing to the floor.

I wasted no time tying him up and then cutting the ties from Mackenzie's wrists and ankles. I spun around to give Mackenzie a high five, but she stopped mid-action. Her face drained of colour.

"What's wrong?" I asked.

Then I saw it too.

23

Plain Bad was showing us he wasn't Plain Bad at all. He stood right in front of the windshield with a gun trained on us. He flicked his gun from me to Mackenzie as if he was deciding who to kill first. Mackenzie yanked me to the floor as bullets peppered the glass.

Oh, how I wished I hadn't underestimated Plain Bad.

Tiny shards rained down. I checked the windshield. The glass must be bullet- and shatterproof because it didn't break. It cracked from edge to edge, but it provided a barrier between us and Plain Bad.

Mackenzie jumped up and slammed the accelerator on the control panel forward. The jolt sent me and Plain Bad flying. She grabbed the wheel and jammed it to the right. Then she cranked it as far as it would go to the left. Plain Bad was shrieking and thudding against the bridge and deck. She zigzagged through the sea at top speed.

"Where did you learn how to drive a ship?" I asked Mackenzie as I was bashed around the bridge like a human bumper car.

"I had a lot of time to study the nav equipment," Mackenzie said, twisting the wheel again. "I'm good with computers."

"Oh," was all I could manage, because my stomach was turning inside out.

"Hold on!" Mackenzie shouted at me. I pounced on the captain's chair and hugged it.

Smack! Plain Bad connected with the windshield and then bounced backwards.

"Aaaarrrrgggggghhhhh!" he cried as he flew off

the deck and plopped on to the slick nose of the ship. He juddered off and splashed into the water. We raced away full speed ahead.

I staggered over to Mackenzie, steadying myself on the control panel. The thrill of surviving was clouded with my overwhelming need to vomit. "Could we slow down?" I asked.

"Oh, um, yeah," she said, seeming to come back to her senses. She slowed the ship to a stop. She hugged me. "Thank you. You didn't have to come back for me. You'd saved my life twice."

When she said it like that, it sounded crazy. I blushed. "*We* did it." Looking at Super Bad passed out on the floor. I couldn't believe we'd actually defeated the bad guys. Maybe I was part criminal and part hero after all.

"Remind me never to make you angry," Mackenzie said.

"Remind me never to let you drive," I replied, and we burst out laughing. We clutched each other and convulsed with laughter. It felt amazing.

Our laughter fizzled into sighs. "I will never be

able to thank you for saving my life," she whispered and absent-mindedly touched the scar on her neck. "I thought you were some goofy American. Was I ever wrong about that! You were bloody brilliant."

"I thought you were some geeky, snobby Brit who'd never eaten a cookie and was preoccupied with manicures and make-up. You need more cookies, but otherwise you're OK." I held her at arm's length. "Are you really a princess?"

Mackenzie shook her head. "My dad is Prince Arthur."

"Are you heir to the throne?" I asked with a curtsey fit for a queen.

She laughed. "No, I'm illegitimate, which means I've got no claim to the throne." She suddenly became serious. "I've never even met my dad. I wouldn't be a welcome surprise to the future king."

And I thought I had parent problems.

We were startled by the ringing of a phone. My brain couldn't process this normal, everyday sound at this anything-but-ordinary moment.

A phone?

"Hello?" Mackenzie answered the phone that was embedded in the control panel. She held the phone between us so I could hear. It was probably the coastguard or the. . .

"C-C-Charlotte?" a voice stuttered on the other end of the line.

"Ariadne?" How could she know where I was and how to call me unless. . .

"Are you girls OK?" Ariadne asked.

"Yes, you should have seen us – bad guys nil, Chase and Mackenzie four!" Mackenzie recounted how we outsmarted and overpowered the bad guys, but my mind was busy putting the puzzle pieces together, and I didn't like the picture it was forming one bit. If Ariadne called the yacht, she had to be mixed up in the heist and kidnapping. Is that why she didn't want me here? Is that why she was so cold to me?

"I knew you girls could take care of yourselves. . ." Ariadne's voice trailed off.

"Ariadne, are you all right?" Mackenzie asked.

It was too crazy to think that my grandma was

one of the bad guys. But what other explanation could there possibly be?

"Yes and no," Ariadne replied after a long pause.

I wanted to say something, but how do you ask your grandma if she is a criminal like her daughter? How do you ask if she tried to kidnap Mackenzie and kill me? I staggered away from the phone.

Mackenzie glared at me in confusion. She hadn't put it together. She was glad to hear Ariadne's voice, the voice of someone she thought was a friend. "Have you called the police?" Mackenzie asked.

Ariadne's reply was simple and told me everything I needed to know. "No, I haven't contacted the police. No one is coming to help you."

Her words hit harder than any blow I'd received today. My own gran threw the knockout punch.

24

I imagined Ariadne ripping off her convincing disguise – the one that made her resemble a nice, but nutty, old lady – and transforming into some evil super-villain, who was half robot and half viper.

"I'll figure out how to use the yacht's radio and call for help," Mackenzie said.

"You can't do that," Ariadne replied.

"What?" Mackenzie exclaimed.

I shook my head. Betrayed by my own grandma. "Don't you get it," I covered the phone's mouth piece and whispered to Mackenzie. "She's in on it. How else would she know how to contact us here?"

"What? No," Mackenzie said, but her face changed as the truth dawned on her. "Ariadne?"

The phone line muffled. We leaned in closer to listen. Someone was with Ariadne. I was sure I could hear two muted voices – Ariadne's and a man's.

The other voice was saying something like "tell them". I couldn't understand exactly what he was saying, but his tone was demanding, not requesting.

"Girls," Ariadne said, paused again, and then shouted, "he threatened to kill me if I didn't trick you to come back to the island, but I can't. Save yourselves! Call for help and sail..." Her words trailed off.

Then came the horrifying sound of a slap and a scream – my grandma's scream.

"Ariadne!" we shouted into the phone.

I had read the situation all wrong.

"Charlotte." It was Artie.

"Is Ariadne OK?" I asked. "What's going on?"

"Charlotte, I need you to listen to me and listen

very carefully," Artie said, his voice as cold and deadly as black ice. Mackenzie and I were cheek-to-cheek with the phone wedged between us. I wondered why he was only talking to me. Mackenzie was the valuable one.

"OK," I replied. He had my complete attention.

"I'm not a bad guy," he said, but a really and truly good guy would never need to say this. "I'm going to offer you a simple trade. Your long, lost grandma for Mackenzie."

I couldn't have heard him right. "What?"

Mackenzie stepped away, leaving the phone in my hands.

"All you need to do is sail the yacht back to the island," he explained. "I will put your grandma in a dinghy and you'll put Mackenzie in one at the same time and we'll swap. You get your granny . . . *ouch* . . . cut that out." Another slap but this time no scream. My grandma was tough, and she hated being called granny. "You get Ariadne, and I get the princess."

"What? No!" I shouted at him. "Why would

Mackenzie ever agree to that?"

I could hear Ariadne in the background shouting, "Don't let her, Charlotte!"

"I don't want to hurt your grandma," Artie spoke louder to be heard over Ariadne's protests. "I've genuinely grown quite fond of her, but I've got a job to do."

"What does that mean?" I asked. "Do you want money? I'll give you money." I didn't know how exactly, but I knew I would find a way.

"You really are a bit thick, aren't you?" Artie said.

I think that was British for stupid, and I was beginning to feel that way.

"I've been hired to kill Mackenzie." He stated this horrible fact without any trace of guilt. "The heist, the bomb, everything was to cover up Princess Mackenzie's murder. How much clearer do I need to make it? If Mackenzie survives today, I'll come for her again – or someone else will."

"What? Why?" I couldn't understand why anyone would want to kill a fourteen-year-old. So what, her dad was the heir to the throne. Big deal.

"I'll keep quiet," Mackenzie interjected. "I don't want anything to do with my father. I want to be left alone. I'm not going to make trouble for anyone."

"I don't make the rules," he said. "I'm carrying out orders and—"

I interrupted. "Orders from who?"

"Enough!" The anger and irritation in Artie's voice came blaring through the phone. "Mackenzie can choose to save your lovely grandmother or wait for the next assassin. Charlotte, I expect the yacht to start moving immediately."

The line went dead, the phone dropped from my hands.

Mackenzie climbed on the control panel and kicked the smashed windshield until it dislodged and crashed to the deck below.

"What are you doing?" I shouted at her. Had she lost her mind?

"I need to see where I'm going," Mackenzie said, punching buttons and pulling levers. The yacht jolted forward.

"Stop it!" I tried to shove her away from the controls, but she held on tight to the wheel. "I'm not going to turn you over to Artie."

"I'm not going to let him kill Ariadne," she said. "Ariadne helped me and my mum when no one else would. I had a near miss with a motorbike in London. The guy came straight at me. If it wasn't for my mum's quick thinking, I'd already be dead. Then someone broke into our flat. My mum scared him off too, but not before he cut me badly enough to send me to A & E." Mackenzie pointed to the two-inch scar on her neck. It was only inches from where her jugular vein would be. "Ariadne agreed to hide me until Mum could figure out who was trying to hurt me and stop them."

I didn't know what to say. She'd already survived multiple attacks on her life.

"My mum was on Prince Arthur's protection detail and had an affair with him before he was married," Mackenzie continued. "She broke it off and got herself reassigned when she realized she was pregnant. He didn't object to her move. They both knew he was never going to marry my mum. They were from different classes, different cultures. Mum never told him she was pregnant. He didn't know about me for ages. When he figured it out, he was furious. We received threats."

"Why didn't your mom have him arrested?" I asked.

"No one would have believed us. He never threatened us directly. It was always veiled threats through back channels." Mackenzie adjusted a few dials on the control panel. "None of this matters any more. He's going to be king one day, and he and his family can't really afford to have me hanging around."

"You can't go through with this," I said.

"What choice do we have?" She kept her eyes focused forward.

"Slow down," I urged. "I'll think of something."

"We don't have time." She kept fiddling with the buttons and knobs. I didn't know how to run this thing or stop her from doing it. "Chase, find a way to call for help. He might be monitoring the radio, so see if there's a computer or mobile phone or something. I'll keep moving."

Maybe help could reach us before I had to choose between Mackenzie and Ariadne.

I raced through the ship and checked every room. I found a laptop in one of the bedrooms on the lower deck at the back of the yacht.

HELP!! I wrote in the email's subject line. I didn't have time to explain everything so I kept the message simple. *Dad, I have been kidnapped and am being held on a yacht right off the island. Please send help! Love, Charlotte*

Charlotte was our code word if either of us was ever in real trouble. He knew I hated being called Charlotte. It was a subtle signal that this was a real threat. Would he see the message quickly enough to make any difference? Would the message even be sent from out here? It was a long shot.

My dad always had a strategy for every situation. As I raced back to the bridge, I wished I knew what he would do if faced with this deadly no-win situation. I didn't care what Mackenzie said, I wasn't going to trade her life for Ariadne's.

I stumbled over something and ended up face down on the deck. I kicked at what had tripped me – scuba diving gear.

And then a wild idea popped into my mind like kettle corn over a campfire. We'd find a way to make it work. I would have to convince Mackenzie that it was worth the risk. I usually loved a risk, whether it was a jump on my bike or a prank on a teacher. But this was different. I was risking other people's lives. It may be the stupidest idea in the history of crazy, wacky ideas – but it just might work!

25

"Are you sure you want to do this?" Mackenzie asked for the millionth time. I'd told her my idea and she'd come up with this brilliant plan. She'd sketched out a diagram on the wall of the bridge and wrote up a timeline.

"Yes!" I snatched the pen away from her. "Stop talking about it, and start doing it."

"You know what you need to do?"

"Yes!" I shouted again, and gripped the yacht's steering wheel until my knuckles bleached white. I had to concentrate on my part of the plan.

"You've told me what I need to know to operate the yacht."

"You realize that our plan is risking Ariadne's life, right?"

"Argh!" I groaned. "Yes, but it could also save both your lives. It's what Ariadne would want us to do." I didn't know Ariadne well, so I wasn't a hundred per cent sure that was true. Mackenzie knew her better than I did.

The phone rang and we jumped.

"Hello," Mackenzie answered flatly. She held the phone between us.

"What's taking so long?" Artie barked.

"You think we know how to drive this thing?" I said. "We're doing the best we can."

"Well, speed it up!" he shouted.

"We can see the island," Mackenzie added.

"Head for the boat dock," Artie said. "Got it?"

"Got it," I repeated. The phone went dead.

"Are you ready?" I asked.

"As I will ever be. In case this goes..." She gulped. "You know, I want you to know that you are the maddest, most brilliant person I've ever met. I would have never survived or had the courage to go through with this without you." She dive-bomb hugged me. I didn't have time to hug her back before she darted away.

"Hey!" I shouted. I wanted to stop her. This plan of ours was mental. Was I really willing to bet their lives on one of my crazy ideas?

"What?" She turned back to me. Tears glistened in her eyes.

"I *will* see you later," I told her. I swallowed to shift the egg-size gumball of fear that was lodged in my throat.

"Yeah," she said as one tear rolled down her cheek. "If not, tell my mum," she wiped at her eyes, "you know."

I shook off the sadness. "We've got to think positive. We won't survive if we don't toughen up."

She puffed up. "Yes, sir, captain, sir!" She saluted me.

I saluted right back, and Mackenzie raced away.

*

I stood on the back deck of the yacht. The same place where only an hour earlier I'd nearly been a shark snack. Artie had called again when he spotted the yacht and told me to stop right where I was. Waiting and watching was way worse than being attacked. All night I could at least fight to survive. Now there was nothing I could do, and this helplessness was killing me.

I zoomed in with the binoculars that I'd found on the bridge and checked on Mackenzie and Ariadne. They were both in dinghies speeding in opposite directions – Mackenzie to the island and Ariadne to me.

I trained the binoculars on Ariadne. Artie had placed her at the front of the dinghy and then set the boat in motion. The waves were knocking her about, and she was springing up and down as if she was in a bouncy castle.

Ariadne's and Mackenzie's boats passed each other. This was the point of no return. Mackenzie kept her focus forward. Ariadne swivelled in her seat to watch Mackenzie. She was screaming something.

"What's she doing?" I shouted even though no one was around to hear me. Ariadne was trying to stand. I adjusted the binoculars so I could see her more clearly. Her hands were tied. She was reaching for the motor. Was she trying to turn her boat around and go after Mackenzie? She didn't know we had a plan. She stood up but the wind and the waves sent her crashing into the side of the boat. If she bounced out, she would drown for sure.

I waved my arms over my head trying to get Ariadne's attention. "Stop it! Stay still!"

Ariadne spotted me right as her dinghy was rocked by the wake from Mackenzie's boat. She knocked the motor, changing her course. She was slammed to the bottom of the boat, which was now heading out to sea.

I untied the remaining dinghy. I had to go after Ariadne. Mackenzie was still rocketing towards the island and Artie. Mackenzie could take care of herself, I reassured myself as I raced after Ariadne.

Ariadne had hauled herself to a sitting position. Her eyes widened in surprise when she spotted me.

She frantically waved at me. "Go back! Save Mackenzie!" she yelled.

Argh! That woman was stubborn. I drew my boat alongside hers. If she didn't stop it, she was going to be tossed out of the boat. "Hit the kill switch!" I screamed at her.

"He's sabotaged it!" she called to me. Artie must have made sure that Ariadne couldn't do anything but jet helplessly out to sea. "I can't shut it down. What are you doing?"

"I'm trying to save you," I shouted back. I reached for her boat, but the moment my hand left the motor, my boat veered away.

I pulled up alongside her again. She'd crawled back to her engine too. "Hold it steady!"

She nodded.

I had to time this right. If I missed, I would end up in the sea, drowned by the waves of the runaway boats – or worse yet, sliced and diced in the blades of the propellers.

Dad always said picture the landing not the fall. I focused on Ariadne and launched myself at her boat. She screamed as my body thumped on to the side of her dinghy. She grabbed for me while my hands scrambled for something to hold. I wrapped my fists around the rope that was strung around the perimeter of the boat. The salty sea was smacking my face while the waves bashed my feet. I skimmed alongside the boat and held on for dear life.

Ariadne grasped one leg. The woman may be old, but she had muscles. She tugged the lower half of my body while I lifted the top half. One final burst from us both and I slipped into the boat.

I tried to catch my breath as my head was repeatedly slammed against the bottom of the boat. It took a second for me to find the rhythm of the waves and steady myself as I crawled to the motor. Something was wedged in the kill switch. I wiggled it free and then flicked the switch. The roar of the engine abruptly stopped, and the boat juddered forward. There was sweet silence, but it only lasted a second.

The air erupted in gunfire. Ariadne and I turned

towards the island in time to see Mackenzie's boat explode.

"Mackenzie!" I lunged in the direction of the blast. An explosion was *not* part of our plan. Ariadne locked her arms around me and held me back.

The flames shot high into the air. Mackenzie's boat was engulfed in a black cloud of smoke. I couldn't see her or the boat or the island.

Ariadne was wailing into my shoulder.

It was as if the smoke and flames gutted me. I stared at the place Mackenzie and her boat should be. I scanned the water for any sign of her. Our plan had gone horribly wrong. I held Ariadne as she sobbed, too stunned to feel anything.

26

"How could you sacrifice Mackenzie to save me?" Ariadne asked.

"We had a plan," I explained in a feeble whisper. "Mackenzie had scuba equipment with her. After you were a safe distance from the island, she would flip her boat and use the scuba gear to swim unnoticed to the Aquatic Centre on the far side of the island. She could steal a boat and go for help."

We stared at the island and the smoky remains of Mackenzie's boat. I don't know how, but Ariadne and I had managed to return to the yacht. We stumbled back to the bridge. Ariadne didn't even blink when she saw Super Bad tied up on the floor out cold. I cut Ariadne's hands free, found blankets and wrapped them around our shoulders.

"Maybe she's OK," I said, desperately wanting to believe it. "We didn't see what happened right before the explosion. We were too busy saving ourselves. Do you think she could have survived?"

"If there's even a slight chance, we must head to the Aquatic Centre," Ariadne said. "Let's hope for the best."

I crossed my fingers and prayed.

Ariadne smiled at me. "Your mother was fearless – and impulsive too."

"Will you tell me more about her?" I asked. If I could survive a heist, bomb, sharks, eels and pirates, I could handle the truth about my mom.

Ariadne hugged me, and I mean really hugged me. "Someday," she whispered in my ear. "For right now, all you need to know is that she would be proud of you. You are a truly amazing young lady."

My grandma thought I was amazing. That was

something. I held on to those words, even though I was feeling the opposite of amazing. "Let's go get Mackenzie."

She ruffled my hair. "Do you know how to run this thing?"

"Sort of." I pressed the buttons Mackenzie had showed me to start the yacht. The engines hummed to life.

I sailed closer to the island, searching sea and sand for any sign of Mackenzie. "There's Artie!" I shouted as if I'd spotted a T-Rex.

"He's heading to the Aquatic Centre too," Ariadne said. "Can you make this go faster? He needs a getaway boat."

Why hadn't I thought of that? I punched the accelerator, and we lurched forward. "Any sign of Mackenzie?" I asked.

Ariadne shook her head. "That doesn't mean anything. She might have made it there already, but if Artie reaches her first. . ."

Neither one of us dared to fill in that blank.

The yacht was difficult to steer, and at its fastest

we weren't outpacing Artie, who was running pretty fast for an old guy. He was going to reach the Aquatic Centre first.

"Hold this!" I shifted Ariadne in front of me and placed her hands on the wheel. "I have an idea." I removed the bullhorn that was mounted to the bridge's wall. It was a lame idea, but I had to do something. I raced on to the deck.

"Stop!" I shouted at Artie through the bullhorn. He stumbled. I cleared my throat and deepened my voice, making it sound manly and forceful like my dad. "We have called the police and the island is surrounded. It's over, Artie!" I'd heard versions of this same line in a million cop shows.

He stopped and turned towards us with a smug grin on his face. Then the strangest thing happened. He raised his hands over his head and dropped to his knees. I was shocked. My stunt had worked!

Maybe this would give Mackenzie the extra time she needed. We had nearly reached the Aquatic Centre. Artie would hop up any minute when he realized I was bluffing.

The yacht slowed. Was something wrong with the engine? I raced back to the bridge to check on Ariadne. "What are you doing?" I asked her.

Tears were streaming down Ariadne's face. She pointed to the sky. What was she trying to tell me? Her words were mangled in her sobs. She kept pointing.

At first I didn't understand, but now I could see. She was pointing at one . . . no, two, three helicopters zooming closer and closer. One had a sniper hanging off the side with his gun trained on Artie.

Another helicopter hovered over Artie and two armed men propelled down ropes and dropped to the ground. Within seconds, Artie was face down in the sand with his hands cuffed behind his back.

I jumped when I heard a thud on the roof of the yacht. Ariadne and I raced on to the deck. The helicopter hovering above us had lowered someone on to our roof. The person was dressed in head-to-toe black and wearing a ski mask. We raced over as he scrambled down from the roof. "Mackenzie.

She's. . . You have to look for Mackenzie," I babbled at our rescuer. "There was an explosion and she's missing. . . Don't worry about us. Find Mackenzie."

Between Ariadne and me, we managed to explain what had happened.

The guy took off his ski mask to reveal long blonde hair. Our rescuer was a woman.

"If she's out there, we'll find her," the woman said. She used the radio that was fastened to her uniform to call and explain the situation. The third helicopter peeled off towards the Aquatic Centre, and one of the men guarding Artie raced in the same direction.

Ariadne and I clung to each other. We were safe at last.

"I'm Chase, and this is Ariadne," I told the woman.

"We know who you are, ma'am," the woman said. "I've been instructed to give you this." She opened a pocket on her uniform and handed me a phone.

"Can you help the rest of the hostages?" Ariadne asked.

The woman pointed out to sea. "More help is coming," she said.

I could make out a ship on the horizon. "There's a bad guy tied up on the bridge and another under the bar at the back of the ship." I'd almost forgotten him.

"We captured four on the island, but there might be others still out there," Ariadne added.

"We'll round them up," she said. "Don't worry."

That's when I noticed the familiar emblem that was embroidered with black thread on her black jacket. She was United States Navy, like my dad.

The phone buzzed in my hand.

"It's for you," the woman said, and she raced off.

"Thanks!" Ariadne called after her.

"Hello?" I answered the phone.

"Chase! Thank God."

"Dad?"

"I got your message," he said. "Are you and Ariadne OK?"

Ariadne was blackened from the first explosion. She had bruises all over her body. I was sure I looked worse. "We're alive."

Ariadne took the phone from me. "You should have seen our girl, Jack. I'm so proud of her. She's fearless. She's a hero. She saved everyone."

When I first arrived on the island, I would have given anything to hear my grandma say she was proud of me. I was *her girl*. None of that mattered any more.

"I didn't save everyone," I whispered and scanned the sea again. There was no sign of Mackenzie.

The survivors rushed to the beach and waved to the ship sailing to the rescue. The scene should have made me happy, but all I could think about was that Mackenzie was either dead or alone. We'd only just met, but after everything we'd been through I felt as if I'd lost my best friend. How did you ever get over something like that?

27

The next day I felt worse not better. Every bone, muscle, fingernail and hair follicle hurt. We were given a medical check by Navy doctors. Ariadne and I needed a few stitches and painkillers. We were flown back to Malé, the Maldives capital, and put up in a hotel overnight. I scrubbed and scrubbed myself in the shower, but I still felt dirty. The doctors gave me something so I could sleep, but my dreams were filled with yesterday's nightmares.

Mackenzie was still missing.

Now we were waiting in a private lounge at the

Malé airport. Ariadne had chartered a jet to take us away from here. With every passing minute, I lost another sliver of hope that I would see Mackenzie again. How could we leave without knowing if Mackenzie was dead or alive? But Ariadne and I weren't given a choice. The Malé authorities and US military thought it was best if we were out of the way. I was lying on a wicker couch and pretending to sleep. It was easier than seeing everyone staring at me with either pity, sadness or suspicion.

Someone draped a blanket over me. It was probably one hundred degrees outside, but I was shivering. From the scent of her perfume, I knew it was Ariadne. She'd spilled her expensive perfume this morning when we were getting ready. The fragrance covered up the smell of the salt, sea, sweat and smoke that seemed to coat us. She was trying to act calm, as if yesterday's multiple near-death experiences hadn't affected her. But I had seen the dark circles under her eyes.

I heard someone else come into the room.

Ariadne walked away. I was too exhausted to open my eyes. They were whispering. That had happened a lot since we left the yacht. Everyone was whispering about me, not to me. How come I was old enough to do what it took to save almost everyone, yet suddenly wasn't old enough to hear what was happening now?

Normally that sort of adult stuff made me crazy, but I didn't want to know anything else. My brain was already full of things that I wished I hadn't seen, wished I hadn't done, wished I'd never known.

I tried not to listen, I really did. But it was as if snippets of their whispered conversation were made of metal and my ears were magnetic.

"Missing, presumed dead."

I never knew anyone my age who had died. I'd certainly never been around when it happened and definitely had never been the cause of death.

"No longer a rescue ... recovery operation."

I rolled over and stared at the cream weave of the fabric on the couch's cushions. In my mind, I catalogued the things that I had done and the people

I'd hurt. *Why* mattered, didn't it? I never meant to hurt anyone. I'd saved way more people than I had hurt. That mattered too, didn't it? But Mackenzie – one of the people who mattered most to me – what had happened to her? Maybe I was more like my mom than I had ever imagined, but it didn't scare me any more. That part of her inside me had helped me survive. At least, I imagined it did.

Someone turned on the TV in the corner of the room. I rolled over when I heard a British TV announcer talking about what had happened yesterday. We'd made the world news. Well, sort of. The news story was about an attempted million-dollar heist. The final image was of the hostages leaving the ship that had rescued us. I recognized the man whose face filled the screen. He was the first guy I freed in the dining hall.

"We owe our lives to a young girl," he was saying.

"I thought the island was for pensioners," the reporter said, and the camera panned to the rest of the grey-haired survivors.

"I don't know who she was, but I know if it wasn't for her, we'd have been killed in an explosion," the man said.

Ariadne was at my side.

The reporter continued, "So a mystery hero and more questions than answers. . ."

"Your dad and I agreed it was best to keep your name out of it," Ariadne said.

I nodded. I didn't care.

Ariadne turned off the TV.

"Don't turn it off!" I shouted and sat bolt upright. "Maybe there's news about Mackenzie."

"There won't be." She sat down next to me.

"What? Why?"

"It's complicated," Ariadne said with a sigh. "The British government has asked that we keep her disappearance out of the news for now. No one knows she was on the island. Only Artie knew her true identity."

"So Prince Arthur sends a hitman after Mackenzie and no one is ever going to know?" I hopped up off the couch. "Well, I'll tell the world. I don't care."

I paced the room. "They have to bring everyone involved in this to justice."

Ariadne led me back over to the couch. "There's no evidence linking Prince Arthur or anyone else to this attack."

"Mackenzie thought Prince Arthur was behind it," I tried to stand. "She and her mom had received threats. Artie said he was working for someone else." Ariadne grabbed my hand. She did the talking yesterday when the police interviewed us. Why didn't she tell them that this was part of a conspiracy to kill Mackenzie?

"Sit down," Ariadne said, patting the seat next to her.

I sat. "We can't let Prince Arthur get away with it. I don't care if he's royalty."

"Accusing the Prince would be a mistake."

"So what if he's rich and powerf—"

"It's not just that," Ariadne interrupted.

"Then what?" Why did adults make everything so complicated? He did something wrong. He didn't do it himself, but he was behind it, which was just as bad.

"Did you hear anyone mention Prince Arthur?"

"No."

"Artie isn't talking, so we don't really know who else is involved. It might not be the Prince."

What was she saying? "Who else would want to hurt Mackenzie?"

Ariadne looked at our clasped hands.

"Ariadne. . ."

"Forget it." She waved her hands wildly as if shooing the idea away. "I'm being stupid and paranoid."

"What aren't you saying?" I stared at her and waited for her to speak. She could see I wasn't going to drop it.

"There may be someone else who might want to hurt Mackenzie," Ariadne said. "Actually, this person's real objective is to hurt Mackenzie's mum."

I suddenly understood what she was struggling to tell me.

"You can't mean Mom. Why would Mom want to hurt Mackenzie? She's in prison. She couldn't possibly be responsible."

"Mackenzie's mum and your mum were best friends from the first day of school." Ariadne settled back into the couch. "They did everything together, but when they got older they..." She paused. I knew she was trying to figure out how to say that Mackenzie's mom dedicated her life to protecting others while my mom hurt people. "They took different paths. Mackenzie's mum and your dad were responsible for catching and convicting your mum."

I felt punched in the gut. "But you said she wasn't all bad."

"She wasn't. She's not." Ariadne quietly added. "I haven't had contact with Beatrice in a long time. She won't see me or respond to any of my messages. I only know the girl I raised. I don't know the person she's become."

My thoughts tangled in knots. None of this made sense.

Ariadne continued in a cold, detached tone. "When you were born and the authorities took you away to live with your dad, your mum knew it was for the best, but she blamed Mackenzie's mum for putting her in prison – for taking away her future with you. She vowed that she would eventually take Mackenzie away from her mum. When bad things started happening to Mackenzie, I was afraid your mum was making good on her threat. I had to protect Mackenzie."

"From my mom," I said, but it was impossible to believe. "So you think Mom was behind this."

I'd found and lost my mom again. I was only beginning to come to terms with the fact that my mom was a criminal. After everything that had happened, everything I'd had to do to survive, I'd grown to understand her a bit more. People had died because of me. It wasn't the same as murder, but I understood that people could do horrible things and not be completely bad people. Could my mom really want to hurt Mackenzie? How could I ever live with that?

"I hope not." Ariadne placed her arm around my shoulders. "I can't believe Beatrice would ever want to harm you or me. I'd hoped she'd found a way to forgive and accept responsibility for what she'd done. Maybe she has. If the police ask a lot of questions, your mum and Mackenzie's mum's past are bound to be dragged up again. I don't want that for you or her. It won't bring Mackenzie back." She pulled me closer.

She was asking me to keep quiet about the larger plot against Mackenzie. She was asking me to protect my mother.

"There is no proof linking what happened yesterday to anyone other than Artie," Ariadne said. "He could have been lying about taking orders from someone. He might have made that up to protect himself. He was probably acting alone. I shouldn't have said anything to you. Your mum is in prison serving time for her crimes. There's no reason to tell the police or anyone about my silly fears. And that's all they are."

I wanted to believe her. My mom couldn't be completely bad. My dad wouldn't have been in a relationship with someone that was horrible. She'd given me life, and she didn't have to do that. She allowed my dad to raise me. She'd stayed away to give me the best chance at happiness. That was something. I'd hold on to the good things about my mom. Until there was proof, I wouldn't believe she'd hurt Mackenzie.

Ariadne hugged me close. It didn't feel strange any more. "Artie and his men have been caught. It's over. We've got to move on."

"Do you think Mackenzie is alive?" I asked. I prayed that Mackenzie was only *presumed* dead.

"Mackenzie is an extraordinary girl." Which didn't really answer my question. "If anyone can survive, she can."

Then that's what I would believe. Mackenzie was out there somewhere.

28

A man in a pilot's uniform walked into the room before I could ask Ariadne anything else. "Miss Sinclair, it's time to board your plane," he said. "Follow me."

We followed.

"I spoke to your dad this morning," Ariadne told me as we headed down a long corridor and on to the tarmac. "He says it's fine with him if you want to stay with me as planned."

The sun's heat was beating down on us and radiating up from the black asphalt. "Really? I thought for sure I'd be on the first plane home to Indiana."

"He said he's proud of you and that you've proven you can take care of yourself," she said with a laugh. "I wanted a little more time to get to know my granddaughter better. I hope that's OK."

"I'd like that, Ariadne." It still felt strange to say her name.

It was as if she read my mind. "Maybe you should call me grandma."

"I thought you hated that word," I said.

"I did." She shrugged. "I'm beginning to see it as a privilege not as a synonym for 'ancient'."

The jet ahead of us was sleek and small. I'd never flown on a private jet before. "Hey, Granny—"

"Don't push it, Chase," she said, giving me a playful bump. She called me Chase. That was a first. Maybe we would get to know each other for real.

"Where are we going?" I asked.

"I'm tired of this sun, sea and sand," she said as we climbed up the stairs to the plane. "I've booked us a flight for a colder climate."

"Some place with no sharks?" I asked.

"Definitely no sharks."

"And no pirates," I added.

"I certainly hope not."

I looked at my shorts and flip-flops. "I'm not really dressed for cold." All my winter clothes were in Indiana.

"Don't worry," she said, stopping at the door of the plane. "I've taken the liberty of ordering you a whole new wardrobe."

Private jet. New wardrobe. I'd dreamed of a life like this. Now it didn't seem so important. Ariadne ushered me on to the plane. It was nicer than my house, with comfy couches, a basket of my favourite candy, jumbo TV screens, and. . .

"Mackenzie!" I shrieked. I couldn't believe my eyes. There she stood with hardly a scratch on her. She looked like the same geeky model I'd met a few days ago. I had never seen anything so amazing in my entire life. I hugged her to make sure I hadn't imagined her.

Ariadne piled on and hugged us. "What? How?" she blubbered through her tears.

"Our stupid plan worked," Mackenzie said with a huge smile.

"Really?" Ariadne and I said in unison. We collapsed on to the couches.

"Yeah, I strapped on my scuba gear, and when Artie started firing at me, I flipped out of the boat and tipped it over," Mackenzie explained. "I was already swimming away when I heard the explosion. I swam straight to the Aquatic Centre. I hid when I heard someone coming, but it was the Navy, not Artie."

"How did you get here?" Ariadne asked.

"Chase's dad convinced the Navy to smuggle me to safety and then sneak me on to the plane," Mackenzie continued. "It's better for everyone if I disappear. Your dad will tell my mum I'm OK, but no one else can know. As long as I'm presumed dead, I'll be safe. You don't mind hanging out with a dead girl for a while, do you?"

That sounded pretty wacky to me.

"You can't get out of helping me launch my *Triple L* app that easily," Ariadne said with a laugh. "Which we're going to do..." Ariadne paused. "Drum roll please."

Mackenzie and I made a sound like a drum roll.

"At the Ice Hotel in Lapland!" Ariadne exclaimed.

"That's where we're going?" I asked.

"Right now?" Mackenzie added.

Ariadne nodded with a big goofy grin on her face.

"We were going there in a few weeks anyway. We are ahead of schedule, that's all. I've got to go speak to the pilot about our flight plan," Ariadne said. "I'll let you two settle in." She exited into the cockpit.

"Can you believe it?" Mackenzie said.

Mackenzie was alive so anything felt possible.

Suddenly I didn't know how to act with Mackenzie. We'd saved each other's lives, but her mom had put mine in prison and my mom may or may not be trying to kill her. Were we enemies or something else?

"Weird, huh?" I said.

"Yeah, completely and utterly bizarre," she replied.

"I'm glad you're not *really* dead."

"That's thanks to you."

We couldn't pick our parents or fix what they had done. But we had each other. She'd proven that she was more than a friend who would help move a body. We'd risked our lives to save each other. I had a feeling this was only the start of our adventures together.

ACKNOWLEDGEMENTS

I'm lucky to have so many wonderful people in my life – people who have made Chasing Danger a better book and me a better person.

Thanks to…

The amazing team at Scholastic. First and foremost to Lena and Sam for their editorial leadership and feedback but also to the artists, designers, proof-readers, publicity, marketing, sales, receptionists and everyone who has welcomed me and my book into the Scholastic family.

My lovely agent Jenny and everyone at Andrew Nurnberg Associates for championing me and my work around the globe.

The other Sara, James and Megan for reading rough drafts and sharing ideas.

To my writerly friends at Book Bound (bookboundretreat.com), on the EDGE (edgeauthors.blogspot.co.uk) and at SCBWI British Isles for their friendship and advice.

To my dad for sharing his love of books in general and thrillers and mysteries in particular. I think he would have liked Chase and Mackenzie. And to all my family and friends on both sides of the Atlantic for their love and encouragement.

And finally to my wonderful husband Paul for loving a woman who plots murder and mayhem while on vacation. You are my co-creator and best friend.

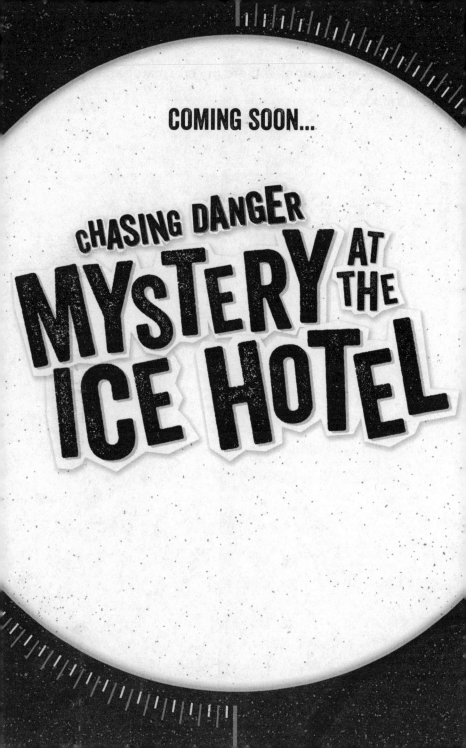

COMING SOON...

CHASING DANGER

MYSTERY AT THE ICE HOTEL